# Wonderfully WRECKED

**RECKLESS BASTARDS MC — MAYHEM, NV**

*WALL STREET JOURNAL & USA TODAY BESTSELLING AUTHOR*

## KB WINTERS

# Copyright and Disclaimer

This book is a work of fiction. The names, characters, places and incidents are products of the writer's imagination and have been used fictitiously and are not to be construed as real. Any resemblance to persons, living or dead, actual events, locales or organizations is entirely coincidental.

Copyright © 2018 Book Boyfriends Publishing

All rights reserved. No part of this publication may be reproduced, stored in or introduced into a retrieval system, or transmitted, in any form, or by any means (electronic, mechanical, photocopying, recording, or otherwise) without the prior written permission of the copyright owner. The author acknowledges the trademarked status and trademark owners of various products referenced in this work of fiction, which have been used without permission. The publication/use of the trademarks is not authorized, associated with, or sponsored by the trademark owners.

# Table of Contents

Copyright and Disclaimer ................................. ii

Chapter 1 ............................................................7

Chapter 2 ..........................................................13

Chapter 3 .......................................................... 33

Chapter 4 ..........................................................47

Chapter 5 ..........................................................55

Chapter 6 ..........................................................73

Chapter 7 ........................................................ 85

Chapter 8 ..........................................................91

Chapter 9 ........................................................ 101

Chapter 10 ......................................................111

Chapter 11 ...................................................... 131

Chapter 12 ......................................................139

Chapter 13 ......................................................159

Chapter 14 ...................................................... 179

Chapter 15 ...................................................... 191

Chapter 16 ...................................................... 205

Chapter 17 ...................................................... 229

| | |
|---|---|
| Chapter 18 | 247 |
| Chapter 19 | 259 |
| Chapter 20 | 269 |
| Chapter 21 | 291 |
| Chapter 22 | 299 |
| Chapter 23 | 308 |
| Chapter 24 | 318 |
| Epilogue | 330 |

# Wonderfully Wrecked

Reckless Bastards MC

By KB Winters

# Chapter 1

*Rocky*

"Tell me what he said, Kody."

I stood inside the kitchenette in my small San Diego apartment, wrapping a bag of frozen green beans around a towel for my friend Kody. Who had a black eye, courtesy of my ex-boyfriend's goons. It'd been two years since I made my escape from the concrete battlefields of Los Angeles and headed for blue skies and rich tourists in San Diego. But suddenly, Genesis and his men were back in my life.

"It's not a big deal Rocky." He sounded like he was spitting out teeth.

My back was to Kody who was splayed out on my couch. For a few moments at least I didn't have to look at the mess they'd made of his face.

"Tell me what happened or I'm putting these veggies back in the fridge."

"You're so damn stubborn. Fine, they told me to *stay the fuck away from Rochelle*. And then *bam* right in the left eye. And the stomach. No big deal," he groaned.

Those fuckers! It was Big Boy and Navajo, it had to be. I'd seen them around for the past couple of months, just watching me. Always watching with those damn smug smirks on their stupid faces. They'd kept their distance after Dallas had threatened their dicks, but only for a while.

"Shit, I'm sorry, Kody. I should have guessed they wouldn't stop."

"You mean shredding your tires?"

"You knew? They'd cost me a pretty penny, slashing all four tires just to inconvenience me. I think they thought I'd get scared and go running back to Genesis. I didn't."

## Wonderfully Wrecked

"Of course I knew," Kody mumbled around his pain. "You're the cheapest person I know and suddenly you have brand new tires on your ten-year-old car. I did the math. And I know about the break-in, too."

Shit. "They're just trying to scare me so I'll go back to LA."

"Will you?" A groan came from the living room and I figured he must've tried to move again.

"Not unless they kidnap me."

Which was probably plan C or D on the list of ways to get me to come back. A bell chimed and I froze, suddenly remembering what I'd been doing before Kody knocked on my door.

"Shit!" I ran into the living room, tossing the towel-wrapped beans at him as I raced to the bathroom and locked the door behind me. My heart beat so loud and hard it was all I could hear as I leaned against the sink. I stared at the five plastic applicators sitting on the counter beside my toothbrush and soap dispenser.

The truth was right there, a few feet away. I didn't want to look, couldn't force my feet to move to see the results. *You can do this. Just open your eyes.* The pep talk didn't work and after counting to ten and back, twice, I took one step. Then another. And then I opened my eyes and looked down at the five different applicators hoping, no *praying* that I wasn't seeing what I was seeing.

*Pregnant. Positive.* Digital displays. One single line and plus signs. They all said the same thing. They all said that my one sexy night of fun in more than two years had left more than a lasting memory. That I was now one of those women who got knocked up by a one-night stand. "Shit." Every time I thought I was making progress in my life, something or someone came along to prove me wrong.

Kody knocked. "Hey Rocky, you okay in there?" I jumped.

"Yeah, I'll be out in a sec." I splashed cold water on my face and stared at the applicators one final time before I swept them into the trash bin. I knew what I had to do. It would start with getting the hell out of San Diego. For a while or forever. But first, I opened the bathroom door and walked into the arms of my best friend.

"Okay. I'm really sorry about bringing all of this into your life, Kody."

"Hey, don't worry about it, Rock. This isn't on you."

He could say that until he was blue in his pretty face, but that nasty purple bruise that closed his eye said otherwise. "It is Kody, and as long as I'm around, they'll make you a target to get to me. I have to leave."

"Where will you go?" He sighed and dropped his head to my shoulder. "I want to talk you out of this so bad, but you have your determined face on and it hurts too much to talk."

I laughed so hard I snorted. "Good because my mind is made up. I'll let you know when and where I land." I would miss Kody. He was the first good friend

I'd had and the fact that he was a guy meant so much to me.

"Wait, what happened in that bathroom?"

"Oh," I smiled and rested both hands on his shoulders. "I'm pregnant."

"The knight in shining armor?"

I nodded because that was what Dallas had been that night. My white knight with messy blond hair, a wide smile and blue eyes that always seemed to be laughing. "Yeah. That one."

I knew Dallas would help me because he had that whole sexy, cornfed cowboy thing going on. But also, because I was carrying his baby.

## Chapter 2

*Lasso*

I was confused as hell and all my Spidey senses were tingling in warning, telling me that shit stunk to high hell and it had nothing to do with the German shepherd next door. Standing on my porch, looking as lush and sexy as she had for one hot night in San Diego, was a girl—a *woman*—I hadn't seen in almost two months.

"Um ... hey Rocky. What's up?"

As I stood there, ready for whatever bomb she was about to drop, another thought occurred. What if Rocky was a stalker? The Reckless Bastards had enough of that lately.

"We need to talk," she said, her tone serious and somber. I braced myself, knowing nothing good ever came after those four words. "Can I come in?"

The way she looked over both shoulders, scanned my residential neighborhood set me on edge and I stepped back, waving her in.

"Are you in some kind of trouble?" Because that would be just fucking perfect. I meet a hot girl and we have one fun night together and now she thinks the big bad biker can swoop in and save her.

"Kind of. Do you have any water? I'm so thirsty but I didn't want to stop for the bathroom so, please?"

All types of warnings clanged around my brain at her words and how they didn't fit together, not with her tone and her actions. But I got her a glass of cold water from the fridge and shoved it in her hands. "There. Start talking."

She didn't look worried at all, just gulped down half the glass and set it on the table, keeping her fingers curled around the bottom.

"Thanks for that. I needed ... oh shit."

One hand smacked over her mouth as her green eyes flashed wide. Worried. She was on her feet seconds later and before I could register what the fuck was going on, Rocky was emptying her stomach in my bathroom. On and on she went, making the most sickening sounds while I stood in my own damn kitchen feeling helpless as fuck.

"Sorry about that," she said when she came out, wiping her mouth with a wad of tissues, the toilet flushing behind her. Her smile was sheepish, her expression contrite.

But now I was on the verge of fucking panicking. "You want to tell me what the hell is going on here?" I refilled her glass and shoved it her hands, forcing her to sit back down before she collapsed on the floor. I wet a kitchen towel and put it on the back of her neck. I didn't know why, I just remember my own mama doing that to me when I made it to the kitchen table with a hangover. "Are you all right?"

"Yes. No. Probably not," she answered softly and then burst into tears, grabbing one of the many scarves around her waist and drying her eyes.

Fuck. Fuck. Fuck.

I hated tears. Nothing made me feel more helpless, more useless than a woman with tears in her eyes. I vowed, after leaving my family and my hometown of Rose Petal, Texas, that I'd never feel that way again. And now, look at me.

Fuck.

All I could do was wrap my arms around her and hold her close while she cried her eyes out, clinging to me and leaving my t-shirt a soggy mess. Thankfully, she didn't have any makeup on so I was just wet.

"Ah shit, Rocky."

She took my words the wrong way, pulling back and sitting tall in the wooden kitchen chair as she wiped away all traces of her tears.

"Sorry. Shit, I'm really sorry, Dallas." She stood, her legs a little wobbly as she walked the few steps to the sink, rinsing out her glass. "Seriously, I'm sorry."

"Should I ask again?" It was obvious she needed help just as it was obvious she didn't want to tell me why. Or ask for my help.

Her southern California tanned skin paled and she shook her head as she sat back in the chair. "No. I'm not dying. Not right now, anyway."

"What the hell does that mean?"

"Remember that guy you saved me from the night we met?" I nodded, how could I forget that neck-tattooed freak with bad hair and worse fucking manners. "He's a henchman for my ex. Ex-employer and ex-lover. Genesis."

I snorted. "Seriously?"

"Yeah. Anyway, he's got a partner and they've upped their bullshit since we last saw each other but at first it was just dumb but inconvenient shit. Slashed tires and a vandalized apartment. I can handle that. I know they thought I'd get scared and go running back to Genesis, but I didn't. But now, they've attacked Kody."

"Your boyfriend?" She'd said nothing about a boyfriend during our night together, but they could have gotten together in the two months since. The thought fucking rankled. It shouldn't have, but it damn well did.

She laughed. "No, Kody is my friend. The first real friend I've ever had, actually, which is why seeing him with a black eye really messed with my head. But Kody is ... great. He's a sensitive guy. A chef with a boyfriend he plans on marrying soon, but it doesn't matter. They've ruined our friendship, so I had to leave San Diego."

An ex who couldn't take rejection wasn't that big of a deal, even if he was a gangster, so none of this told me why it was my door she'd knocked on. We'd hooked up in San Diego but that was months and miles ago. This was Mayhem, close to Vegas. Not that big of a jump but definitely not San Diego. Again, I wanted to know why she landed on my doorstep.

"Because, Dallas."

I winced at her use of my given name. No one ever called me Dallas. Hell, I didn't even know why I introduced myself to her like that. The name was a reminder of everything I'd left behind, everything I hated about home. Family. "Lasso. Call me Lasso."

Red brows rose dramatically. "Considering what that says about me, I'll pass. Anyway, I had to leave because who knows what they'll do now, and my situation changed about the same time Kody showed up with his black eye." She sighed, wringing her hands in the fabric of her orangish-pink skirt. "I'm pregnant, Dallas. It's yours but that's not why I'm here. I just need…just…a few days to make a plan."

*Pregnant? Pregnant. Pregnant?* The word sounded in my head until it had absolutely no meaning, other than what it meant for my life. My future. She was still talking but I'd stopped listening. I just watched her lips move but the sound didn't register. Lush pink lips moved, occasionally her fingers ran through thick red hair but otherwise she just talked.

"I know this is a lot to take in, Dallas, and I'm damn sorry for that, but I was acting on instinct. I don't need money. I just need to lie low for a few days. No one knows you who could connect us. Please." Her brows dipped low and her shoulders fell. Resignation.

"You're pregnant?" Words finally came and they were...idiotic.

"I am. You're the only man I've been with in two years, but like I said, I'm not asking for anything else. Not cash, not your belief, or your protection other than a few days' safety of this place nobody knows about."

"How long?" The words came out harsher than I meant them to, but it was the first thought that came to mind.

She sighed, disappointed but again, resigned. "Right. Maybe a week or two, but let's just say three days? Can you give me three days?"

Shit. What the hell kind of shit was she involved in that she wasn't cursing me out for not offering more help? She said she was carrying my baby. Shouldn't she be demanding my protection and my financial assistance? "Is this a scam or some kind of game?"

## Wonderfully Wrecked

"No," she laughed bitterly. "It's neither of those things but you don't know me to know that. I get it," she said with a casual shrug that told me she did get it. Her green eyes were sad but determined as she finished her water and stood. "See you around, Dallas."

No. Hell no. There was no way I'd fall for this trick. This little game meant to tug on my emotions. Good thing I didn't have any emotions because I didn't trust anyone but my brothers. A few of the old timers were married, some had permanent old ladies and even some of my friends had gotten loved up, but I didn't trust women. I liked them, but when the time came that they dicked over my brothers, I'd be the first in line to make sure they paid the price.

Still, I felt like an asshole. She was pregnant and had an angry ex after her, and I was turning her way. *But what if she isn't pregnant?* That was the question my conscience kept poking and prodding my brain with. The practical side of me wanted to know what if she was, and that thought had me on my feet at the front door just in time to see her pull the door open on an old black Chevy Blazer with matted paint. "What kind of trouble are you in, exactly?"

She didn't turn around, didn't look up at me to try and plead her case one final time. If this was a game, giving up wouldn't get her anything, would it?

"Do you need my help?"

She did look up then and what I saw was fatigue. And fear. Her gaze slammed right into me, blank and bright green even from fifty feet away. "Nah, I'll figure something out."

"Where are you staying?"

Her smile was sad, wistful even. "Wherever I stop next."

She hopped in the Blazer, started the ignition, and pulled away. Exiting my life just as quickly as she'd entered it.

Except this time, she was carrying my kid.

Probably.

Maybe.

# Wonderfully Wrecked

Shit. I had to go after her.

***

I'd caught up to her at a burger joint and convinced her to come back to my place and we were finishing up a meal I'd thrown together. "The car," I asked, "is it stolen?"

She screwed up her face in a show of indignation. "No, it's not stolen. I'm not a car thief. But I took the long way here, stopping to trade my car in for something a little bigger and a lot less conspicuous." She was right, the red Mini Cooper she had on the night we met was an eyecatcher, but the redhead inside? Impossible to ignore.

"What are you running from exactly?" She'd said an ex had sent his men after her. Henchmen, she said, which meant he was more than a low-level gangster.

"I already told you. Goons who want to drag me back to a life I already left behind." The way she sighed and her shoulders slumped reminded me of my own demeanor when I left Texas for the last time. She scraped every last bit of sauce and cheese from the lasagna on her plate, and then rinsed it in the sink, readying herself to say something. "I appreciate the dinner, Dallas, I do. But you don't have to do this."

"Do what?"

"Pretend you care. I dropped all this in your lap unexpectedly and you've handled it like a champ, but you don't owe me anything. I'm sorry if I made you feel like you did."

Goddammit, this girl was determined to make me get in touch with my sensitive side. "I don't do anything I don't want to, Rocky." Including her.

"Right," she said and pushed my hand away as I slid a plate of chocolate cake in front of her. "Stop trying to feed me if you want me to believe you're as tough as you appear." But she sliced her fork through a corner, bit it and moaned low and deep.

"And don't try to distract me with that sex moan. Just tell me what I want to know."

"My *what*?" She choked as she swallowed another bite.

"That sex moan. Believe me, I remember." Her cheeks turned an adorable shade of pink, especially considering all the dirty shit we'd done together that night.

Rocky rolled her eyes and pushed the plate away. "Okay, the short version is that my dad is—or maybe was—a bank robber. We learned one day a long time ago that I had a knack for planning heists, which meant I had no choice but to do them with him."

I poured her a glass of milk to go with the chocolate cake and let her roll out the story.

"At first it was fun, you know, drawing up plans and spending time with my dad. But then it became a job and two months before I turned seventeen, I left Florida behind. Hopped on a bus, stopping here and there to wait tables and gather more cash for wherever

I landed. When I got to California, it was my first taste of freedom." She inhaled deeply. "It was so intoxicating, all the sunshine, which I was used to, but the freedom. It was great!"

She smiled and for a moment she looked like the sexy redhead I'd met on the beach, looking hotter than anyone should in plain black slacks and a fitted white shirt.

"I know a little something about that," I said. "After the military I went back to Texas and my family and their oppressive fucking expectations. When I made my escape, it was to here. There was no ocean but that smell and that feeling of freedom. Yeah I know exactly what you mean." It was like being released from prison or gaining eyesight for the first time.

But I was interrupting her. I apologized and told her to tell me the rest.

"So I was waiting tables and selling my crafts on the beach when I first met Genesis. He was good looking and he had that charm that really young seventeen-year-old girls find appealing, and I was a *really* young seventeen year old." She rolled her eyes with that self-deprecating smile that brought back memories of our night together.

"I didn't realize what he was at first. I mean, my dad was a crook but not *that* kind of criminal, at least I didn't think so. Anyway, I realized what kind of man he was when I owed him some money and had trouble paying it back."

"Your own boyfriend?" I shook my head. That guy was a fucking asshole.

"Yep. See, a few of us were getting together for a bachelorette party and I thought it'd be nice to have a little pot for the night. But Genesis said this was a grown up party and that I should bring coke. I'd done a line here and there but nothing real serious. He offered me some so I took it. It wasn't until the next day he told me I owed him $1200. 'Ass or cash,' he said."

Her gaze darkened as she relived the memory and my fingers itched to pound that fucker's face into the cement. "Then a few days later he magically remembered how I used to help my dad."

"Wait, what? Seriously?"

She just nodded sadly.

"What a fucking prick," I said. The guy was an asshole, but he was smart to take advantage of such a fantastic and hidden talent.

"Yeah, but after the first heist went so well, my debt was cleared. You can imagine my relief. But then he started to pay me. Cash, zanies and vicos," she said, casually tossing out the street name for Xanax and Vicodin.

"I had this little one-bedroom apartment with plenty of light in the living room. My craft room was my living room and I had this long table by the balcony where I had an almost unobstructed view of the Hollywood sign."

She sighed wistfully, her green eyes someplace else, that happier time I assumed.

"I was in a happy bubble, stoned and crafting, planning two or three heists a month for a fat bundle of cash. I kept doing it, not even thinking about it at all, Dallas, not until I gave up the pills."

"Why?" I needed to know if I had to worry about having a junkie in my house and carrying my kid.

She shrugged. "I was over it and I preferred the way I felt with pot, a little spacey but not enough that I could ignore my conscience. And I started thinking that if I was going to do this with my life, I could at least be with Dad." A laugh erupted out of her. "Okay, so not really the short version, but there it is, the whole story."

I reached over and fingered a few crumbs from her plate, licking my thumb before I said, "And you think that's why he wants you back?"

She rolled her eyes, swiped her phone screen a few times and shoved it under my nose. I frowned at the room on her screen, filled with bins of yarn, tubes of glitter, fake flowers, beads and plenty of other shit that the old ladies in Rose Petal would love. "What the hell am I looking at?"

She laughed but the sound was harsh and bitter. "My prison. Genesis wanted to keep me high and planning heists for him while I did my crafts. Whether I wanted to or not."

"And you're not tempted, not even a little?" If she was going to change her mind in a few days, I couldn't get involved. If I landed myself in the middle of some on and off couple, I would send her on her way right damn now.

"Hell no. I mean, I get why he might think I'd come back, but I'm not the girl too naïve and too blind to see the truth anymore. And honestly, there's nothing quite like being on my own."

"No, there isn't." The desert air made it easier to breathe than the thick, suffocating air in Rose Petal.

"So yeah, I'm not going back. But I need a plan and to make a decent one, I need time. For some reason, I thought you might help, but it's okay if you won't. I always land on my feet."

Shit. I couldn't let her go now, knowing she was pregnant with a gangbanger after her. "One more question, who does this Genesis run with?"

Rocky stood and grabbed her bag, heading for my front door again. "The Killer Aces. See ya, Lasso."

# Chapter 3

*Rocky*

Two days. That was how long I'd been at Lasso's place and I wouldn't even start with how I felt about him insisting I call him by that ridiculous nickname. But I obliged because he was nice enough to let me lay low and invade his space for a while. And I still didn't have a good plan to start a new life someplace else, though I was waiting to hear from a guy I used to know about a new identity.

Other than staring at blank paper and crafting, I was bored out of my mind. Terrified about my uncertain future as a single parent. Even now, I sat on the shaded back porch, knitting an oversized sweater that was a commissioned order, and hoping my phone wouldn't ring. I'd changed numbers twice since I left San Diego and this time, Genesis hadn't been able to get it.

Or he was biding his time.

Either way, the sooner I came up with a plan for my future, the faster I'd be out of his reach and safe to worry about the rest of my life. Which for the immediate future meant dealing with another outlaw biker. I'd seen Lasso's leather jacket and insignia, and knew I was in danger of repeating my past mistakes. There had to be a sign on my forehead or maybe it was a scent, that said I was a magnet for outlaws.

It was a good thing I wasn't hanging around long enough to make too many mistakes.

The last mistake had nearly cost me my life after a night of grief, pills and booze, and now I had someone else to worry about, so I had to be smart. My kid needed me to be better than I was right now, better than my dad had ever been and better than my mom was before she walked out when I was three. I'd have to do more with my online craft store, make more money to take care of me and a baby and find a place to live. Hell, I had to find a state to live in, then find a doctor and buy baby clothes and beds and stuff. I needed baby books and vegetables. They were good for growing fetuses, weren't they?

"Hey, hey Rocky! Breathe." I turned, shocked to find Lasso right in front of me, on his knees, his big blue eyes looking hella concerned. "Breathe in, two three, and out two three four." He repeated it two more times and I followed along until my heart, that I hadn't even realized was racing, began to slow down.

"Thanks."

"What's wrong?"

"Nothing. Just feeling a tad overwhelmed for a minute." It was an understatement, but the telltale pulse at the base of my throat said otherwise.

"By just sitting here?"

"No," I told him and rolled my eyes in frustration. "Thinking about my future and making plans, okay? Jeez, I'm fine."

Can't a girl freak out about her future without everyone going a little crazy? I didn't need Lasso to try and figure me out. Men only wanted to get into a woman's head for two reasons, to fuck us or control us, and I wasn't in the market for either of those things.

"You've been sick a lot." His words were said plainly but something about them just put me off.

"Yeah well, if they called it all day sickness, women might make better birth control decisions." The really twisted part of all this was that we had used birth control. "Too bad no one tells you antibiotics cancel out the pill until it's already failed. The bastards."

His blue eyes bugged out. "No shit?"

"No shit," I said and let the conversation die because it was obvious Lasso had something on his mind. "What are you doing back so early, I thought you were at the tattoo shop until eight?" He looked embarrassed and wouldn't look at me.

I knew what it was about. I'd had the same thought about a few roommates before I'd finally gotten my own place. I stood and picked up my basket of yarn and my sticks, making sure I kept all of my shit in the tiny guest closet he'd let me use. "I'm not going to steal your shit, Lasso. But I'll leave with you in the morning and spend the day someplace else until you come back." He followed me to the closet where I put my things away and grabbed a book. "I'll be out of here in another day or so."

"Where are you going," he asked, frowning at me from the doorway because he was too damn big to even fit in this room.

"I don't know yet, but I'm working on a plan and in a few days, I'll have it as close to perfect as it can get."

If there was one thing in this life I did well, it was make plans. Logistics.

He sighed, arms crossed so his t-shirt pulled across a wide, muscled chest and thick, round biceps. "I didn't say you had to leave, Rocky. You should do something about that chip on your shoulder before it squashes you."

Maybe he was right. I probably did have a chip on my shoulder, but it was well fucking earned. "You didn't have to say it, you were trying very hard not to say it. But this is your place, and no one should make you feel uncomfortable in your own home. Least of all me."

"I don't know what the hell that even means, but it sounds to me like you're trying to kick up shit."

Of course, it did, because I was a hormonal female and every emotion I had wasn't because he was a suspicious dick, but because I couldn't control my emotions.

"I have no control over what you think. Now if you don't mind, I think I need to rest." I closed the door in his face, climbed onto the small twin bed and promptly fell asleep.

It was as fitful as all of my sleep had been for the past two weeks.

\*\*\*

## Wonderfully Wrecked

I woke up early, grabbed my purple yoga mat and took it to the quiet solitude of the early morning. The only sounds this time of day were birds chirping and singing back and forth, presumably about where they would fly for the day. I tried to get up early and do yoga at least two or three times a week because it helped me stay grounded.

Today I needed it with a capital N thanks to another night of disturbingly delicious sex dreams featuring a man named Lasso mixed in with dreams of what my future would look like if Genesis got his hands on me. Again. I woke up at four and hadn't been able to get back to sleep. After two hours of staring at the ceiling, I got up and slipped into my yoga clothes.

I'd been standing upright for at least thirty minutes without any trace of nausea or the urge to vomit. Either morning sickness was over, or I'd confused my body enough by getting up a few hours earlier than normal. Whatever the cause, I accepted it with nothing but gratitude.

It might not last all day though. So I finished up, rolled up my mat and set it beside the door, and went inside to rustle up some breakfast. This small bit of freedom from nausea meant I could actually enjoy breakfast. I pulled out spinach, eggs, salsa and avocado for the biggest, fattest omelet my belly had seen in what felt like ages.

With a big, greedy smile I sat down and dug in.

"Damn, something smells good in here!" Lasso's bare feet hit the bottom of the steps with a loud smack, his wide, lazy gait eating up the kitchen floor. "Please tell me you made enough for two?"

"Didn't think you'd be up yet." I didn't really know what time he got up though, because I'd planned to make sure I was long gone in case he thought I was trying to lift a few of his precious possessions.

He frowned at me and drank the coffee that had brewed on a timer. "What are you doing up so early?"

"Couldn't sleep," I answered around a mouthful of omelet.

## Wonderfully Wrecked

"Everything okay?" His voice was filled with concern, but I shrugged it off because the last thing I needed was to see that big sexy outlaw cowboy staring at me like I was his something special.

"Yep. Just restless."

If he was bothered by my short answers, he didn't show it. Just flashed that panty melting smile and leaned back in his chair, sipping his coffee. "What are you up to today?"

I savored the last bite with a little bit of everything on the fork, chewing slowly because I'd made it through a meal—through breakfast—without getting sick. It was a sweet moment that ended with a scowling biker.

"Just running a few errands and mailing a few orders. How about you," I asked automatically, still the polite southern girl at heart. Yeah, right.

"Fine." He pushed up from the table and grabbed his coffee before he stormed from the room.

If I didn't savor being a bitch once in a while, I might have felt bad about that. But I couldn't find my give a damn, so I cleaned my dishes and went upstairs to get everything I'd need for the day. Including cash for a visit to the medical clinic in town, just in case Genesis was much smarter than I gave him credit for.

A few plans played out in my mind as I loaded up the Blazer and got on the road, but for one reason or another, they all ended the same. With Genesis and his thugs finding me, making me pay and then locking me up to be their little dancer monkey.

I pulled into the parking lot of the family planning clinic, parked in the middle of the lot and looked through the rearview mirror just in time to see a familiar vehicle roll right past me. Checking up on me.

There was no time to worry about Lasso because it was time for my first official doctor's appointment and I was nervous as hell. Not that there was anything for me to do, really, other than getting probed and interrogated. The difference was there was a baby in there, growing and taking nutrients from me. It was bizarre. But by the time I got up on the crinkly exam paper, my nerves had settled a bit and I was excited to know more.

"Well?" I said to Dr. Hanson.

She had a kind smile and soft brown eyes, somehow understanding the gravity of my situation enough to take a moment before she answered.

"You're about eight weeks along and everything looks normal. I have a prescription for prenatal vitamins. Take them every day and be sure to eat a healthy, balanced diet. Some things may give you heartburn like onions, pizza, spicy foods. Stay away from alcohol and beer. No smoking. Come back and see me in six weeks or if you leave town, call so we can forward your records to your obstetrician."

When she asked if I had any questions, I just stared at her like a deer caught in the headlights on a dark road. I had a million questions, but I couldn't remember a single one.

"Stress!" I just blurted the word out rather than ask a question, but Dr. Hanson smiled.

"Try to keep your stress to a minimum. It'll be good for you and the baby, just remember that."

How could I forget? The mixed scents in the waiting room had brought my nausea right to the forefront of my day which meant deep breathing through the doctor's visit, the trip to the drug store to fill the prescriptions and pick up a couple cases of ginger ale and plain wheat crackers. Also, a little bit of junk food because I wanted to be prepared.

Inside the bookstore, the troublesome scents were the strongest with coffee as the aggressor. I held my breath and quickly perused the pregnancy books. My dad was a good provider but stunk at being a dad. He had no patience or time for things like play time and nurturing unless it would help with his next score. With no role models, I needed all the help I could get. I settled on three different child care and pregnancy manuals before I passed out from holding my breath.

It wasn't much better outside but at least I could breathe. I felt like I'd driven all around the town of Mayhem and parts of Vegas, stopping at the grocery store, bakery and craft store before heading home. It was a long day and I hoped Lasso would be home soon so I could go to the guest room and crash.

I waited ninety minutes for him. When he didn't come home I bit the bullet and went inside, leaving my bags beside the bed as I curled on top of it. I remembered one final task before I could finally sleep.

I needed to send Lasso a text.

KB Winters

## Chapter 4

*Lasso*

**Hope you got your answers. ~R**

That was it, just five words and it had me spooked and a little bit curious about how a little redheaded hippie chick could have spotted my tail. I'd even taken my truck so it wouldn't be obvious because I was damn curious where she was going that required such secrecy. Maybe I was overreacting. She wasn't secretive; Rocky just wasn't sharing any information with me.

Goddammit!

And the worst part was, I couldn't even blame her. I made her feel unwelcome to the point she spent all day out of the house, pregnant and doing who knew what, all because she misinterpreted what I'd said. But seriously, would it have been so hard to just say she was going to the doctor? I drove past and parked on the street, watching her in the rearview. She looked like she was freaking out or trying not to before she stepped from the car and walked inside on shaky legs. Then I pulled away, picked up my bike and went to meet the guys at the clubhouse.

I asked a few of them to meet me there to work out a solution to the problem of Rocky's crazy former boss and ex-boyfriend. When I pulled up to the clubhouse Cross waited around the back where customers weren't allowed. I walked up and he handed me a cold beer.

"A little early for a beer isn't it?"

He shrugged, leaning back on the wooden table Gunnar had a few of the prospects put together last summer, a sweaty green bottle hanging from his fingertips. "Never too early for beer and this isn't even the strong shit."

I took the bottle and drank in silence for several long minutes, trying to make sense of this shit. Rocky had been with me for three days and I hadn't found out any more information than I had on the first damn day.

"Remember that redhead chick from San Diego?"

"The best night you ever had? Even better than that night in Kiev?"

"Yeah. Well, she's about two months pregnant with my kid and on the run from her ex."

"Shit." That was Cross, talkative as ever.

"Yeah and she's not asking me for anything but a few days to come up with a plan, but I can't just let it go at that. I have to help her, and I hope that means you guys will help too."

By the time I finished speaking, Savior and Max had come out, along with Golden Boy, Jag and Stitch. Gunnar was still handling personal business and the rest of the guys were taking care of club business.

"Man, this shit is serious." Jag stepped forward with his hands shoved deep into his pockets. "I know of the Killer Aces. A cousin of mine in Long Beach said these fuckers are crazier than regular crazy. Genesis didn't make it as an Angel of Reckoning, so he put together a bunch of assholes too crazy for any other MC and created Killer Aces. They've taken over Southern Cali with brutal efficiency."

Shit. That's the last thing I wanted to hear because I could hear what no one had said yet. What they were all trying damn hard not to say, and that bitter irony twisted in my gut because Rocky had said the same damn thing to me.

"So that's it, then?" I looked around at my friends, my brothers, and they all looked sorry. "I'm not going to let him take her prisoner and definitely not with my kid!"

"*Maybe* your kid," Savior clarified. "For all you know she just figured you were the perfect guy to protect her and a fake pregnancy would make you more eager to help."

"There's still a big damn chance it's mine. You'd leave your kid to that fate? You think that shit is right?"

Savior shrugged. "Yo man, it ain't about right and wrong. It's about war. Bloody fucking war, man. All for some chick none of us know at all. Risking our lives, the club, for a fucking stranger?" He shrugged again, his gaze deadly serious. "It's us or it's her and I'm choosing the Reckless Bastards every goddamn day of the week, twice on Sunday."

My throat constricted and acid made my gut turn over as reality settled over me like a hot, suffocating blanket. "Everyone agrees with him?" A few of them, Max and Golden Boy, nodded because they didn't want their women caught in the crossfire of a war. Others just looked away, unable to even look me in the fucking face.

*Fucking cowards.*

I shook my head, disappointment and anger boiling inside me. I'd gone to bat for every one of these fuckers, put my life on the line. Hell, my soul, too, with the shit I've done. And they weren't even willing to consider helping me. Or my damn kid.

Suddenly I had to get out of there before I said something I wouldn't be able to take back. Hell, the way I felt then, I might not want to take that shit back. So I stood and my feet got to moving, putting more and more distance between me and them. Of all the things I'd expected on my way to the clubhouse, this wasn't even on my list of possibilities.

For the first fucking time since I put Rose Petal and the expectations that came with that huge plot of land behind me, I was on my own. What a sick, twisted fucking irony.

"What aren't you saying?" Max's deep voice stopped me, but I didn't turn around. I couldn't fucking look at him.

"Nothing, man. Don't even worry about it." I kept moving, walking toward my bike and backing it out of the spot, waiting for Max to speak. "Spit it out, Max."

"You know, if she was your girl—"

"Yeah," I cut him off and held up my hands. "I fucking heard it the first time." I understood the need for caution. Reckless Bastards hadn't gone to war with another club for years, but that didn't mean not protecting Rocky and the baby would be okay. It wouldn't.

## Wonderfully Wrecked

Max sighed and stepped in front of my bike with his massive arms crossed over his wide chest. "I know there's something you're not saying man, so just spill it."

"Nothing to say. Not that it would matter anyway, right? Club can't have war. End of conversation," I shouted over the sound of the engine starting, grabbed the handles and swerved around him, taking off out of the clubhouse parking lot. Away from my brothers in arms, my family.

I needed space and time and distance. There was only one thing I needed when my mind was so muddled like it was now, letting my bike stretch her legs on the open road. After about twenty miles, the white noise left. At thirty-five miles, a bit of clarity came.

At the fifty-mile mark, it became crystal clear.

If my brothers weren't going to help me, I'd have to do it myself.

KB Winters

# Chapter 5

*Rocky*

"Fucking piece of shit!" Genesis figured if he couldn't get to me in real life, he would fuck with me through my online store, placing order after order with ominous messages on them. They were all some variation of the "mine" theme he was going with. *You're mine* or just the more threatening *Mine*. Embroidered, hand-stitched, knitted or crocheted, he requested it all.

And I did what any businesswoman in her right mind would, I canceled the orders and refunded his money because I knew exactly what the rat bastard was up to. He thought he could trace me, knowing I'd never complete his order. But what he didn't know or perhaps didn't realize, was that I'd learned a lot in the sixteen months since I'd called him my boyfriend, and one of the things I'd learned early on was that a virtual private network meant no one, not even Genesis, could track me online.

"Ma'am, are you all right?"

I looked up at the pretty middle-aged librarian who smiled at me with concern in her violet eyes. "I am, thank you. Just a client with unreasonable demands. I'll keep it down." I probably wouldn't keep it down, because Genesis had wasted hours of my time sifting through his phony orders and the air conditioning in the library could use a serious upgrade. "Sorry."

"No problem. Thank you for your patronage."

That pulled a smile from me. "I actually have a box of books from a recent move. Would you be interested in them?"

Her smile lit up as she gave me information on donating books to the Mayhem Public Library and it was just enough to make me forget about my own life. For a minute, anyway.

I gave a friendly wave and made my way back to the Blazer and groaned as the leather seats singed my skin. It was too damn hot in the desert and I knew that wherever I moved next, it wouldn't be a place that was all heat and no wind. I was forced to do the one thing I didn't want to, go back to Lasso's house, even though he wasn't home yet. I hated to do it, but it had to be done, so I made a compromise with myself. I stayed on the sofa with my laptop and a giant plastic case of beads and worked until my fingers and my back ached and sweat dripped down my neck.

Eventually hunger called and roused myself from the sofa to make something to eat. I just hoped like hell I would be able to keep it down. Yesterday I'd gone grocery shopping, so I pulled out mahi-mahi, asparagus and mashed potatoes from the refrigerator and forty minutes later dinner was almost ready and still no nausea in sight.

"Thank all the goddesses in the sky!" I whispered as I wiped down the counter.

"Interesting." Lasso's deep voice scared the shit out of me.

"What the hell?" My heart thudded so loud and so hard, I had to catch my breath. "Stop doing that."

He smirked. "Aren't you supposed to be keeping an eye out for bad guys?"

He was right of course, the bastard. "Yeah, well, silly me, I thought I was safe here." That wasn't fair, of course, but I didn't give a damn. I shook off my annoyance and piled the fish on a plate and put it on the table with the rest of the food. "There's enough for two if you're hungry and don't worry, I bought this myself." He hadn't said anything yet, but I knew he didn't want me here and I was determined not to be a burden.

"I wasn't worried. And I told you to stop this crazy shit, leaving while I'm gone. It's fucking stupid."

I gave him a cold stare and took a seat before I served myself. "Your opinion," I said and then started to eat, slowly in case the baby decided he or she was no longer hungry.

"You look upset, want to talk about it?"

## Wonderfully Wrecked

"Nope." Genesis was a problem I couldn't avoid, but my disappearance had given me time to come up with a foolproof plan. "You?"

"Not even a little."

"Great." I stared at him for a long moment and he stared back at me, our eyes connected the way they had when he was buried deep, plowing me to an indescribable pleasure I'd never felt before. But that was Dallas, a handsome, charming and gorgeous man who'd stepped in to help me. It wasn't Lasso, a hardened, cold biker who was grumpy and didn't want me around.

I preferred Dallas, but I was grateful for Lasso because he was the alphahole who'd make it easy for me to walk away in a few days.

***

MINE FOREVER. Fuck. It was another message from Genesis, disguised as an order for an oversized blanket this time and this time I had a decision to make. I needed to decide if I would pull the trigger on the only viable plan that had come together over the past week. A new identity, a new look and a new town. It'd have to be far from here just to make sure I didn't accidentally run into anyone I knew. And it meant saying goodbye to the few friends like Kody I'd made over the years.

Fucking Genesis. He was determined to ruin my life if he couldn't be part of it or benefit from it. Asshole.

The idea of erasing myself completely didn't sit well with me, but then again, I didn't have much in this life to hang on to anyway. And this was the only option that didn't end ten or twenty years later, with me right where Genesis wanted me. I just needed to let the idea sit another day before I decided what to do. I shut down my computer and lay back on the Adirondack chaise that I'd rescued from the shed behind the garage.

"We're going out to eat. Get dressed." Lasso stood tall, casting a long shadow over me.

Wonderfully Wrecked

I stared up at him with a blank look, amazed a man so large was able to move so quietly and pissed that he thought he could order me around. "Was that an invitation? Because it needs work."

"It's not an invitation. We both need to eat and this tiptoeing around each other like something is gonna break isn't going to work." Arms crossed, he looked determined.

That was his problem, not mine. "You don't need to tiptoe around, Lasso, this is your home."

"Maybe, but right now it's *our* house and it's damned uncomfortable."

I nodded my head because he was right. Those rare occasions we were here together were tense and silent. Uncomfortable, as he said. "This is your home Lasso and you've been kind enough to let me stay. I really appreciate that. But, I'll be out of your hair tomorrow."

It wasn't ideal since I'd already given myself a deadline to put a plan into action, but I could probably find a sublet that wouldn't require me to use a credit card or my social security number.

"Goddammit Rocky, you are the most infuriating woman I have ever met!" He raked both hands through his thick blond hair, blowing out a long, pissed off breath as he began to pace the porch behind me. "I'm not asking you to leave."

"You didn't have to," I reminded him. "I was always going to leave."

"Where will you go?" He stopped and dropped down beside me, looking at me with concern.

"I haven't decided yet, but once I'm gone, Lasso, that's it. You won't see me, see us, ever again." I stared at him for a long time to make sure he understood what I was saying to him.

Those blue eyes that most often were the color of the sky, darkened to midnight blue as he unfolded his big body until he stood, towering over me once again. Trying to intimidate me. "Don't fucking play games with me, Rocky. I won't be manipulated or guilted into a damn thing."

I was surprised by his outburst, but it helped my decision. "Good to know." Standing, I stretched my aching back and now that Lasso was here, I went inside and closed myself up in the guest bedroom, stripped down and settled down for a nap.

A minute later, Lasso burst in, burning with anger. "What the fuck is your problem?"

I pulled the covers up to my neck and sat up on the bed with a sigh. "You, apparently. What's wrong now, Lasso? I'm leaving. I'll be out of your hair soon. Your life can go back to the way it was and yet you're still unhappy. Do you want me to terminate the pregnancy, is that what all of this is?"

He wouldn't be the first guy to go a little crazy at the thought of impending fatherhood, and he certainly wouldn't be the first to pressure a chick into ending a pregnancy.

"What? No! Why would you even ask me that?" His chest heaved, his skin was flushed, and I must've been a sick and twisted bitch, because I was instantly turned on. Wet and ready for another night with Lasso before I never saw him again.

My brows arched at his question. "Fine, Lasso. Tell me how I'm the bad guy now."

"What the hell do you mean I won't see you or my kid again?" I could see the rest of the words perched on the edge of his mouth. *If it really is my kid.* He wanted to say it, but good manners wouldn't allow it.

"What do you think it means? The only chance I have to survive this is to disappear completely."

He frowned, the grooves between his brows growing deeper with every passing second. "I don't like it."

So much for a late afternoon nap.

"Turn around," I said.

"What the fuck for?"

"I'm not going to stay in this bed all day and I don't have any clothes on. Now turn the fuck around."

He did, making sure I saw a little smirk around the corners of his mouth first.

I slid off the bed and grabbed a long, peach colored dress. It was gauzy enough that I wouldn't pass out from the heat and it was nice enough I could go wherever I wanted and right now, I just wanted peace.

"I'm not asking you to like it. You don't want me here anyway and soon, I won't be your problem," I said as I slipped the dress over my head. When I was dressed I tried to push past him, but Lasso held a tight grip to my arm.

"I never said I didn't want you here."

"You didn't have to," I told him and tried again to yank from his grasp. "Let me go."

"No. We need to talk about this plan of yours."

"No, we don't. It's my life and my plan. I asked you for a place to lay low, that's it. I already have one asshole trying to run my life, I'm not in the market for another." With those evil words, his hand released me.

"That's what you think of me?"

I didn't answer him, I was too angry to even deal with him. I walked into the living room and plopped on the couch, I could barely slide my feet into my gladiator sandals because my hands shook so badly. When I finally got them on, I stood and found myself face to broad chest with Lasso. "I don't think anything of you, Lasso. I don't know you, but I am grateful for the help. Now if you don't mind, I have some things to do."

"Actually, I do mind." Both hands wrapped around my arms and pulled me close. "No one tells me what to do yet every time I turn around, you're trying to tell me how it's gonna be."

"That's what happens when a woman has a brain. She doesn't need some man to come in and fix her life."

He growled at me, an honest to goodness fucking growl. It was hot and bossy and alpha, and it shouldn't have turned me on as much as it did. But before I could think about what that said about me, his lips were on mine in a fevered, frenzied kiss that had no start or end to it, just a long simmering heat that had finally exploded.

One minute we were fighting, arguing about life and death, and the next we were kissing each other like it was the only thing giving us life. His hands gripped my ass and lifted me in the air, my legs automatically wrapping around him as though they remembered exactly what to do. His body was big and commanding, hard as steel as he moved in closer. The heat between us grew by degrees with every pass of his tongue over mine, every sweep of my hand through his hair.

"Dallas," I moaned in his ear as his mouth skidded down my neck and across my collarbone.

"Fuck, Rocky," he groaned when one hand left my ass and slid around to rub along the wet spot between my legs. "You're already wet for me."

He was right, I was. I ached to have him buried deep in me again, thrusting and pushing into me over and over, pushing me farther than I ever thought I could go. Giving me more pleasure than any man ever had.

"What are you gonna do about it?"

His grin turned dark and playful as he slipped a finger into me without any hesitation. He didn't play or tease, just slid deep until I felt my body clench around him. "Fuck, you're so tight." His words were guttural, intense and he looked ready to snap.

Good, that was just what I wanted. I knew it was just what I needed to happen before we said goodbye. "It'll be even tighter wrapped around you." My whispered words made him shiver and he thrust harder and faster, determined to wring an orgasm out of me before he gave in and slipped me his cock.

But Lasso was the kind of man who didn't shirk on his partner's pleasure, which was why my body already lit up like Fourth of July fireworks as he moved me closer and closer to the first orgasm. "Come on, Rocky. Let me see how fucking sexy you look when you come apart. Show me."

## Wonderfully Wrecked

His words and his finger pulled the orgasm from me with the force of an invading army, stripping me of every defense as my body gave in to the pleasure. The undeniable rush and satisfaction of a much-needed orgasm. "Dallas!" That was it, one word. Just his name as pleasure swamped me.

And then I was sliding down his body until my feet hit the carpet, my legs barely able to hold me up without Lasso's arm tight around my waist. He shucked his jeans, tossed his shirt aside and sat on the sofa. "Come here." He crooked his finger and I swore to God, it was the sexiest fucking thing on the planet.

Like the good little girl I wasn't, I went to him. I let him tug my panties down my legs and watched him inhale the scent of me. I lifted my arms so he could remove my dress and settle me on his lap. His cock was long and hard, wetness already gathering at the tip.

Imposing.

Delicious.

Wicked.

His big hands grabbed my hips and slid me up and down his shaft until he was coated with my juices. "Fuck, you feel that? How much you want this cock?"

There was no point denying his words, but I wouldn't give him the satisfaction of admitting to it, His ego was big enough. But I wanted this because who knew how long it'd be before I found another man I trusted enough? A life as someone else, a single mom someone else, would be hard enough without adding romantic entanglements to the mix.

I took his thick cock in my hand and leaned forward to kiss him, lowering myself on his erection while my mouth fucked his, slow and hard. "Yes," I moaned when he was finally buried deep. It felt so good, so right. My body quivered with every thrust and I knew my next orgasm was imminent.

"Rocky," he groaned, grabbing my hips hard and moving me in a harder, harsher rhythm that made my whole body rejoice. He pumped hard and fast, taking me on a trip into the heavens and back before finally, blessedly, the dam broke.

## Wonderfully Wrecked

My body shook and convulsed, tightened around him like a vise as I rode out my orgasm, and pulling Lasso's out in the process. "Yes!" I collapsed on top of him and moaned. "Damn, I missed that."

His laugh was deep and amused, no doubt his ego suitably massaged. "No shit. You're a hell of a woman, Rocky." I didn't believe that for a second, it was just one of those things guys felt the need to say in the aftermath of sex. But I didn't need pretty words or fake promises filled with false emotion. I just needed this.

"How about we see if we can make it to the bed for the next round?"

I would enjoy this night with Lasso, make it last for as long as possible and then tomorrow I'd wake up and reach out to the ID guy and then I'd get my ass on the road so I could get settled somewhere before the baby was born.

KB Winters

# Chapter 6

*Lasso*

I woke up with Rocky's soft ass in my hand and my cock hard and ready for more of what I'd gotten on and off all night. Soft, willing woman. Pliant woman. Adventurous woman. Ravenous woman. She'd been hungry for me, for the pleasure that ignited between us whenever we touched but I was sure she was hungry for something more. The way Rocky fucked felt a lot like goodbye and I didn't like it one damn bit. Her back was to me, exposing the tattooed thorny stems crawling up her spine and her breaths came deep and even as she slept.

I wouldn't let her push me away. As soon as she was up, I'd force her to talk about what she planned to do and what I could do to get her to let me help. But for now, I needed a shower and food. What I really needed was another round with Rocky, but she looked too peaceful to disturb, so I grabbed my clothes and headed to my bedroom.

The sound of a motorcycle drew my attention in the early morning quiet of the residential neighborhood I lived in, made up mostly of young working professionals and a few families. We never heard bikes here. I wondered what was up.

I stepped into my jeans and pulled a tee over my head, greeting Savior barefoot on the front steps. "What's up man?" I wasn't in the mood for company, but I had an idea about why he'd show up this early.

He lifted a hand in greeting and dropped down on the top step. "Look Lasso, you're our brother and we want to help you out here. But we can't. Not for some chick you don't even know who's *claiming* to be pregnant with your kid. I know you probably don't want to think about that shit right now but with what you're asking, we have to ask."

Yeah, they *had* to ask. "Bullshit. My word suddenly isn't good enough? Good to know." I knew the club had a hierarchy and I accepted it. I'd gone to battle

## Wonderfully Wrecked

for my brothers on more than one occasion and I would do it again and again to protect my family. But now that I needed them, there were all these fucking conditions on that help. That's *loyalty*?

"Come on, Lasso. If Genesis is determined to have her, he'll stop at nothing. That means war, Lasso. Fucking war."

No one wanted war. Despite what all the shows and movies sold as a story, war was bad for everyone. No one came out the other side without battle scars, mental and physical, as well as plenty of fucking loss. Lives and money would have to be paid before the war ended. It'd be fierce and bloody. But how could they avoid it when the risk was losing Rocky and my kid? "So, what are you asking here? Get a DNA test and maybe you'll consider helping Rocky, is that about it?" I pushed off the wall and groaned. "Thanks for letting me know."

"Don't do anything stupid, Lasso."

"You mean don't do anything stupid while wearing my *kutte*, right?" Because at the end of the day, no matter how much we protested our similarities, the guys in the Reckless Bastards MC were caught up in the same bureaucratic bullshit as the military. "Don't worry, Savior. The MC's rep is safe from me." I let the door slam on my way back inside, stomping through my house on my way to the shower as the anger rolled off me.

I could've asked him to reconsider but I knew it wouldn't fucking matter. The one lesson my old man taught me that actually stuck with me was that begging didn't strengthen the rightness of your position, it only made you look weak. It let the other person know how much something meant and that was usually right when they took it away.

Either way, you were fucked. In this case, the people getting fucked would be me and Rocky. And my kid. If I didn't figure out something. Fast.

***

## Wonderfully Wrecked

Work. Just like back on my family ranch in Texas, work was the best way to forget all the bullshit occupying real estate in my mind. GET INK'D was exactly where I needed to be. Permanently inking some skin or stabbing some holes through people would allow me to work through some plans for keeping Rocky safe. My family had houses all over the world, any of which we could use.

If I went crawling back to my daddy and probably agreed to join the family business. And that was a nonstarter. That meant moving on to plan B.

"Hey Lasso, who pissed in your coffee this morning?" Jag walked in with a wide, pearly white smile and two cups of coffee in his hands.

"Savior," I grunted and accepted the cup, relishing the scalding hot liquid.

That was all the explanation Jag needed. He nodded thoughtfully, as usual, before he spoke. "Do you think this baby is yours or do you have doubts?"

"At first I was skeptical as hell, some random chick I fucked one night shows up on my doorstep saying she's knocked up and it's mine. I'd be crazy not to, right? But she didn't, hell she still doesn't want anything from me. The only thing she's ever asked for was a place to lay low while she formed a plan." Saying the words out loud made me feel like a special kind of asshole. Pregnant and afraid and it never even occurred to Rocky that I might have more to offer. "You know why she came to me?"

Jag chuckled. "Because you're a Reckless Bastard and she knew you'd protect her?"

I laughed because that would have been better than the truth. "Nope. Because no one knows who I am or her connection to me. I'm the perfect head start for her new fucking life. She thinks I'm gonna let her leave with my kid."

"Can you stop her?" Savior asked.

Shit, I didn't know. I raked a hand through my hair, trying to get rid of some of this fucking frustration any way I could. "No, but I have to try."

## Wonderfully Wrecked

"Or…" Jag continued. "You could just let her stay a few days like she needs and let her go. Why get involved at all?"

"Because that's not my fucking style, man. Could you let a kid of yours just be out there in the world and not be there for them? Protect them?" Yeah it might make my life easier, but I carried around enough regrets in my life that I didn't need to add abandoning my own fucking kid to the pot. Knowing there are crazy assholes chasing her to make her some psycho's slave? Could you do that?"

Jag shrugged. "For a chick I'd fucked once? Maybe?" But his dark eyes told the truth. He could talk a tough game, but Jag was the best of us.

"Bullshit," I said and finished off my coffee.

He smiled his boyish smile that made all the ladies come running. "Yeah, okay so I couldn't. But I had to make sure you were solid."

"Rock fucking solid, brother." We bumped our fists and cleaned up our shit, separating to our stations to get ready for the day. Ever since Golden Boy opened the place, it was never quiet. There was rarely a dead minute at the shop and today, that was exactly what I needed.

"What do you think you'll do?" Jag's gaze was clear and sober, offering up the support no one else had.

"Whatever I can, I guess. She's stubborn and doesn't trust anyone."

"Sounds like Teddy," Golden Boy said as he peeked his head out of his office, smiling like the lovesick fool he was. "She came by it honestly. While I was busy mistrusting her, she didn't trust me either."

I didn't know what he was getting at and I didn't care. His story only reminded me of how the club had rallied for Teddy before she was even his girl. I mean sure, we all knew she was his before he realized it, dumb fuck that he was, but…dammit. I couldn't go there, not again. "I need to get my shit ready."

## Wonderfully Wrecked

"Everything cool with you, Lasso?" Golden Boy's tone was even but I heard the note of steel shot through every syllable.

"Yep."

He frowned and I could tell he didn't believe me, and he shouldn't have because I didn't even try to hide how I was feeling.

"Good."

"Great."

We were bullshitting each other but I was done, disappearing behind the privacy screen to make sure all of my tools were how I liked them. When the first customers of the day arrived, a pair of old hippies getting matching wedding ring tats, I got down to business, answering questions on autopilot and just focusing on the work. It was an endless stream of vibrant colors and all black ink jobs, fraternity and sorority ink, hummingbirds, skull & crossbones and every fucking thing in between. The day passed quickly, but not quick enough.

I was damn grateful when the last customers left and Jag locked the door, leaving us to clean our stations and leave the place looking like less of a pigsty. Golden Boy had checked out earlier, eager to spend time with his new baby and woman.

I didn't even want to think about him because I couldn't, not without getting pissed off and not without wanting to do my brothers physical harm. "I'm out of here. See you around, Jag."

"Call if you need to talk, or if you need help handcuffing her to the radiator." He smirked like he was the funniest fucker in town.

"Thanks, Jag. For nothin'." He wasn't far off though. I knew it would take an act of God to get Rocky to listen to reason, to get her to see that staying with me was the best choice for her safety and the safety of our kid.

I knew I'd need plenty of ammo just to make her listen and made a few stops to get flowers, chocolate, ginger ale and crackers, plus other things I thought might make her more open to listening.

## Wonderfully Wrecked

As soon as my bike came to a stop in the driveway, I knew something was wrong. The house was pitch dark like no one had been there for a long time, but I unlocked the door and went inside, calling out for Rocky.

No fucking answer.

Still, I checked the empty guestroom and prayed that maybe she'd moved her shit to my room since it was bigger, but she wasn't there. The tiny guestroom wasn't just empty, it was bare and possibly cleaner than when she'd moved in. In the kitchen, among the loot I'd picked up at the store was an envelope with my name on it in Rocky's slanted whimsical handwriting.

***Thanks for your help. ~R***

That was it. No phone number or hints about where she might go. No details and not even a fucking goodbye.

KB Winters

# Chapter 7

*Rocky*

Damn this pregnancy business was exhausting, and it seemed to have its own damn schedule that I could either stick to or face the consequences. Today I had to face the consequences since my plans to get out of dodge had been pushed up to *right fucking now*. I woke up early this morning with a smile on my face, expecting to roll over and smile at Lasso, maybe wrap my arms around his neck and pull him close for a little early morning wake up call.

Instead, the sound of two masculine voices sounding fucking serious grabbed my attention. Lasso and one of his motorcycle buddies sat outside talking and they hadn't been very discreet about it, not that they needed to be. Neither of them owed me a damn thing and the minute I'd heard they agreed, I knew my time here was over. I couldn't expect Lasso to upend his whole life for me, a virtual stranger, and a kid he probably didn't want. I was used to it, being discarded when I was no longer useful. Hell, since Genesis was the only one who wanted me, maybe I was running in the wrong direction?

"Yeah, right." I couldn't even let myself start thinking like that. It was defeatist, and it would end up with me in a position I didn't relish: at Genesis' command.

That couldn't happen, so I kept my foot on the gas, pushing towards an unknown destination. I'd hopped on Interstate 15 and drove, hoping to make it to I-80 before I was too tired to keep driving. Which could be any minute now, or in nine hours. It was up to the baby, apparently. As long as I made it to the small town on the Nevada-Arizona border to get my new IDs, I'd consider anything more than that a win.

But first, I needed food and caffeine, so I turned into the first drive-thru I spotted and loaded up on grease and fat and salt. I was pretty sure pregnant women were supposed to avoid caffeine, so I opted for a milkshake and water to go with my pregnant lady's feast.

My phone rang as I sifted through my purse to pay for my meal and like a fool, I answered without looking at the display. "Yeah?"

"What the fuck, Rocky?"

Lasso. "Could you be a bit more specific? Actually, don't. Let's not do this since I don't have time at the moment so I'll just…yeah." It wasn't the most eloquent conversation but my goal was to get him off the phone before he tried to get me to reveal my whereabouts. He called back, twice and I ignored both calls, grabbing my food and finding a parking spot with a clear view of the street so I could dig in.

The phone rain again and I screamed into the empty car. "What?"

"What the fuck?"

I let out a frustrated sigh. "I'm not doing this with you, Lasso. Tell me what you want or stop playing on the phone."

"I'm playing? You tear out of here like a bat out of hell and I'm the one playing games?"

"Oh please, give it a rest. I heard you and your biker buddy this morning. I'm not taking a fucking DNA test and I don't recall asking for your goddamn protection!"

"Yeah well, I'm offering it up anyway."

"Thank you Lasso, but no thanks. You don't owe me shit. Go back to your friends and your club and forget you ever met me." That was what I'd try to do and I knew it would be hard. Lasso and I weren't some great love story, but he was a decent guy who'd stepped in to help me when I needed it. "Seriously, thank you. For everything."

A knock on my window startled a scream out of me and I looked up at the intruder with the wide, cocky smile and serious blue eyes. "Why do I get the feeling you're trying to get away from me, sweetheart?"

I sighed. "Because you're more than just a pretty face?"

"That might be true," he wagged his finger playfully, "but I won't be distracted so easily, so tell me what in the hell you were thinking?"

Who did he think he was? "How did you find me?"

"One question at a time, Rocky."

I growled. "Yeah. *Mine*. How?"

He shrugged, and it was so damn infuriating I wanted to start the engine and run over his damn feet. "Your location is on, probably because of the GPS."

I dropped my head onto the steering wheel, smacking my forehead against the center and causing a small beep of the horn. "Why did you follow me? Are you trying to get me killed?"

"You know I'm not. I don't give a damn what you think you heard me and Savior say, I'm going to keep you safe."

"I'll keep me safe, thank you very much."

I wasn't trying to be a bitch, but I stood a better chance on my own.

"Must you be so damn stubborn, woman? That's my baby you're carrying in your belly which means it's up to me to keep you both safe. I don't care if you like it, Rocky, not one fucking bit. I care that you and my kid are safe. Got it?"

Did it make me a weak slut that his tough guy, alpha forcefulness got me just a tad hot and bothered again? Because it did. More than a tad. But that wouldn't be happening anytime soon, not with such a high-handed jerk.

"Whatever," I told him and rolled the window up, determined to finish my meal in my last moments of peace because I knew Lasso wouldn't let this go.

He'd probably toss me over his shoulder and force me back if I tried to resist.

In the end, it was safety. Plain and boring safety, and not the reckless, hot lust that overcame me at the idea of Lasso tossing me over his shoulder acting all cave-man that made the decision for me.

# Chapter 8

*Lasso*

Hours after I'd asked Jag if he could track Rocky's phone, we both made it home, exhausted and cranky. "Your bed is too damn small, just sleep in my room." I didn't mean to bark at her, but I'd been up since sunrise and in a few hours the sun would be up again. I was beyond tired and I didn't feel like arguing. Luckily, Rocky had finally decided to stop fighting me. At least for now.

She picked up the small duffel bag without a word and dropped it on the floor beside the bed. "I think I'll take a shower now," she said.

Rocky stood in her wrinkled cotton tank and tiny denim shorts, grabbed her bag and disappeared into the bathroom and locked the door behind her.

I didn't know what I expected from her, but it wasn't this stony fucking silence. Maybe I thought I was owed gratitude but she gave me nothing. Reluctant acceptance and nothing more. It took me nearly an hour to unload all the shit from her car and when I went back to the bedroom, she was asleep.

On my side of the bed.

But she was there and that was what mattered, at least that was what I told myself the next day—and the day after that. But on the third day I came home and couldn't find her. Again.

"Rocky!"

It wasn't like my place was huge; it was just four bedrooms, two floors with a front and back yard so it wasn't like she could be lost. She had to be gone.

"Damn woman," I grumbled as I went to the bedroom we now shared, not that anything remotely sexual was going on, and found it empty.

Ready to blow my lid, I pushed open the guest room door and was met with the back of Rocky's head and a mostly bare back thanks to the shirt held together by nothing more than a few strings. She didn't hear me with her earbuds in and I took advantage of the moment to watch her.

Rocky was a beautiful woman, a bit too bohemian with her wild red hair and colorful wardrobe that reminded me of those sexy Woodstock chicks from the sixties. She bopped her head to the beat, humming along as her hands made quick movements around the white fabric covered with double-stemmed cherries.

Though she still seemed upbeat, everything about her had been subdued since I'd tracked her down just past the Nevada border. She turned, gasped and nearly fell off the tiny fucking stool that I knew wasn't mine. "What the fuck?"

I stood up straight. "What's wrong? Is everything okay?"

"For fuck's sake, Lasso. You damn near gave me a heart attack!" She scowled up at me, waiting for an answer. "Well, what's the problem?"

"I didn't know where you were," I admitted, owning up to the fact that I sounded like a pussy-whipped asshole.

"You thought I was gone, didn't you? Well I don't know what to tell you. I guess you're just gonna have to trust me."

I scoffed at that. "How in the hell can I trust you? You already ran once."

"I didn't *run*, I left just like I told you I would when I landed on your doorstep. And I'm not *asking* you to trust me. Either do, or don't. I don't give a fuck." With her arms crossed, she was a beautiful picture of defiance.

"Trust is earned."

"Or it's taken by force," she shouted, standing and damn near stumbling over the billowy skirt that was tangled up in her tiny blue stool. "I'm here Lasso. I don't want to be but I am so I don't know what in the hell else you want me to say or do, but I'm here. You won. Get over it or whatever, but I have work to do."

## Wonderfully Wrecked

"No, you don't."

I don't know why in the hell I was being such a dick to her, but I couldn't seem to help myself. Trying to pull the fabric from her hand proved difficult because Rocky was stronger than she looked, and she was pregnant so I didn't want to risk hurting her. My gaze narrowed at her triumphant grin. "Working is an unnecessary risk right now."

"And it also happens to be how I make my living, at least until I get settled somewhere, so I'm not stopping." There was a fear in her eyes, one I'd seen on women and children in the desert. It was wild and ready to pounce at the first sign of danger.

I crossed my arms and leaned on the doorjamb. "Are you okay? Have you gotten any more messages from Genesis?"

"No."

I believed her, which meant she was in denial. "And why do you think that is, Rocky? Do you think he just gave up?" She opened her mouth and I pushed off the wall and got in her face. "Or maybe he just has other people buying shit for him *from you* so he can see where you are? Or maybe they keep placing orders so he can make sure you're still in the same place."

I saw the moment real fear flashed in her big green eyes. Then resignation. "Shit. I never gave him credit for being that smart."

"Survival means being smart, Rocky. The prick may not be a genius, but he runs a criminal organization and he's managed to avoid jail time so he's no idiot."

She nodded, but the way she nibbled her plump bottom lip told me she was more afraid than she let on. "He wouldn't have gone through the trouble. Would he?"

"Is it worth the risk? I can cover you until this blows over and you get back on your feet." It was an offer I never thought I'd hear myself make to any woman but that was probably because of all the moneygrubbing socialites my mama had thrown at me before I ducked the hell out of Rose Petal.

## Wonderfully Wrecked

"No offense Lasso, but I can't risk all of my baby's stuff being confiscated because of your dubious earnings."

I had to laugh before I remembered that Rocky didn't know about my family; most of the club didn't even know.

"Dubious? I work in a tattoo shop owned by one of my brothers, in addition to a stake in several dispensaries, whorehouses and the biggest, baddest gun range in Vegas. It's all legit. Feel better now?"

She shook her head, looking even angrier now than before I tried to soothe her fears. "No. I don't like this. We're practically strangers and we don't trust each other. I won't take any money from you. Nope. Not happenin'."

"We won't be strangers because we'll be living and sleeping together, which means we'll grow to trust each other. I'm going to trust that you won't poison me or run off with my shit."

"And I'm going to trust that you're not as bad as the guy I'm running away from?"

I smirked at her smart mouth. Despite her hippy dippy outer shell, Rocky was tough. She was scrappy and that was sexy as hell. "For now, I just need you to trust that I can take care of you and our kid for as long as you need me to, okay?"

I couldn't believe I had to convince her to *let me* take care of her. In my experience that was what most women were looking for, at least the ones I knew. The Reckless Bitches wanted to become someone's old lady, random chicks wanted the bad boy biker persona to make them feel better about the boring accountant they'd left at home, and the rest of them were looking to land a rich husband.

"No! It's not okay, Lasso. Nothing about this is okay. I can't be dependent on you…I can't." Tears began to pool in her eyes and I got nervous. "Just forget this, okay? I'll find another way to work."

"Rocky, no. Here," I pulled cash from my pocket and peeled off a few bills before handing them to her.

"That's seven fifty, more than enough for you to feel like you're not dependent on me okay?"

Another rejection was poised on the tip of her tongue. Instead, her gaze took on an inquisitive glint. "Why? Just tell me why this is so fucking important all of a sudden?"

"It's not all of a sudden, goddammit! You're not the only one who needed time to think, Rocky. We're having a fucking baby and that is huge! There's no way in hell I can let you walk away and not know where you'll be or how you're both doing."

Her pale, freckle-covered shoulders slumped as my words sank in. Then she straightened up and hit me with a sledgehammer. "And if I decide to terminate?"

"What? Are you thinking about that?" I already thought she was firm about keeping it.

She opened her mouth ready to tell me the lie that would get her out of here, paused and then snapped it shut again. "No."

"I'm not trying to control you, Rocky. I just want to keep you safe from those fuckers."

She scoffed. "The baby. You want to keep the baby safe."

I frowned, not understanding the goddamn difference. "Yes, I do, and that means keeping you safe, too. Are you going to fight me on every little thing?"

"What would be the point? You'll just strongarm me to get your way, anyway." The stiff set of her shoulders said that was what she absolutely fucking believed, that I would disregard her feelings in favor of my own.

"Good," I told her, standing tall and flashing my sexiest cowboy smile. "Because I think we should get married."

# Chapter 9

*Rocky*

Married? He thought we should get married?

I squeezed the trigger over and over, three, four, five, six, seven times until there were no more bullets to fire. With the nine-millimeter clasped between my hands, I did exactly as the biker who'd helped me said. Max was his name.

*Aim. Breathe. Fire. Married.* I reloaded and squeezed again. Each and every damn time the word popped into my head, hovered on the edge of my mouth, I squeezed that damn trigger. Not that I wanted to hurt Lasso, I didn't. He was a good guy who I'd put in an impossible situation. *Married.* Like that would just fix everything. *Married. Married.*

"It makes sense," he'd said like it would make me feel better about my wholly emotional and completely irrational feelings of hurt and rejection.

"This way you can take care of all the baby stuff under my insurance."

Just what every woman wanted to hear. How romantic. *Squeeze! Squeeze! Squeeze!* "Put me on the birth certificate," he'd said like that required a fucking priest and government forms.

When the final bullet left the gun, it took the last of my anger right along with it. What was the point in being angry about it now? I was hormonal and would be for the next few months. But married? Like he was the type to stick around forever. Like he wanted a life where he got up in the middle of the night to change diapers or go to little league games or play tea party. Because those were the simple, normal, boring as shit things I wanted for my kid.

"Just think about it," he'd said. Like I would think about anything else for the next few days just because he told me to. It wasn't very smart on his part to spring that on me and then send me off to a gun range, but then again, Lasso probably thought I should be jumping for joy at his offer.

## Wonderfully Wrecked

I knew he was right about Genesis tracking me down, and I hated that it hadn't crossed my mind that all the tweens and hipsters and old ladies who bought my stuff could be friends of his. It was a rookie mistake, which was why I agreed to come to the gun range today, though right now I was regretting it.

The more I thought about his offer, the angrier I got. If I ever got married it would be because I found a decent man and fell in love with him. Not because he knocked me up and not because it was a practical decision. I'd already compromised too much.

No more.

After a quick reload, which, by the way, was the best part of shooting, I took a deep, calming breath and aimed the way the gruff Max had instructed. If the time came and I had to shoot for real, I wanted to be the one to survive. Soon the good old pregnancy fatigue set in, and I went through the checklist as fast as I could, eager to get home before I started to nod off.

"Thanks for the lesson, Max."

"You're welcome." His quiet, grey eyes held a wealth of emotions, but he was stoic as ever. "Did you need something else?"

"Yeah, the bill."

"Don't worry about it," he insisted dismissively and that just pissed me right off.

"The bill. Please."

He didn't look happy about it, but he punched a button and a receipt spit out, which he thrust at me angrily. "You don't have to do this, you know."

I knew exactly what he was talking about and that sent my anger right up to pissed the fuck off. I shoved some cash into his hand and glared because seriously, who the fuck did this guy think he was?

"Yeah, well, after your *brother* tracked me down and forced me to come back here, I'd say that was a matter of opinion, except I never fucking asked for yours. Have a good day."

## Wonderfully Wrecked

I couldn't get away fast enough. Literally because another man clad in leather and denim was strolling my way.

I sped up.

"Hey, wait up!" There was no way in hell I was waiting for that guy. "Hey, Rocky, right?"

"Nope, you got the wrong girl, buddy." There was no way I was putting myself in front of another angry biker who thought I was trying to swindle their boy. I hopped in my car and sped away and promised never to come back. I kept my foot on the gas until I turned into Lasso's driveway and dragged myself up onto the porch and to the bed I now shared with him.

I couldn't be sure since I was half asleep, but I remember picking up the phone to heavy breathing. Three times.

***

"How long?"

I woke up to Lasso with his big beefy arms folded across his expansive chest, those blue eyes glaring down at me.

"Excuse me?" My brain was still foggy and I blinked to bring his angry face into focus. "How long *what,* exactly?"

"How long have you been getting these fucking hang-up calls, Rocky? Were you even going to tell me about them?"

"How did you find out?"

"I answered your goddamn phone; how do you think? Waiting on you to talk to me is pointless, isn't it?" He raked a hand through his hair and dropped down on the bed beside me. "I need you to help me out here, Rocky."

"There's nothing to help with. I was half asleep when those calls came in and I didn't know if I was dreaming or not. And stop answering my phone!"

"That's what you're worried about right now?"

"You want me to trust you and then you do shit that makes it damn hard to do that, so do you want to play this game?" I sat up and pushed my hair out of my face. "And I don't need your damn friends weighing in on my life. I didn't ask them or you for help."

"What are you talking about?"

"Nothing. Don't worry about it. Are you done yelling?"

"I'm not yelling. I'm being firm."

I laughed. "Yet I am not a horse or a dog." He looked properly chastised, but I wasn't buying it.

"Okay, fine, but you can't keep shit like this from me." He sounded tired and worried, reminding me once again that he was a good man.

"Fine, I won't. But if you ever wake me up from a nap when it's not an emergency, I promise this will be the last baby you ever have." Even though he laughed, I meant it. "I've been sleeping like shit lately despite the fact that I feel like all I do is sleep."

"Fine. I didn't realize you weren't sleeping well."

He really didn't get it and I couldn't be upset about that. "There is a human growing inside of me, Lasso. My hormones are fucked up and make me feel like I'm insane, and then suddenly I get so tired I can't keep my eyes open so, yeah, let me sleep."

He looked at me for a long time after my outburst was finished and then Lasso burst out laughing. A full-bodied, deep-throated laugh that was so contagious I had to fight the urge to join him.

"I didn't realize it was that bad," he said, tugging playfully on my arm. "Let's go out to dinner."

I blinked. "Are you fucking bipolar?"

"No, why?"

"Dinner?"

He nodded, his overgrown curls bouncing and making my fingers itch to run through those blond ringlets. "Yes, dinner. A meal people typically eat in the evening sometime after lunch. Let's go out and feed you properly."

## Wonderfully Wrecked

I was about to tell him it wasn't necessary, but my stomach interrupted the conversation. "Don't say one damn word and I'll go freshen up right now." I pointed my finger in his face and watched his incredible show of willpower as his lips twitched with mirth before he finally gave in.

"That wasn't a word. Make it snappy and I'll even let you order my food so you can pick from it too."

Ugh, when Lasso was full on good ol' boy charming he was impossible to resist. I could feel my body responding to him and I wished I could control it.

"You really are a good guy, Lasso. Even with the unfortunate nickname. It's too bad we didn't meet some other time." The twist in my gut told me how much I wished that were true. Good guys were a rarity in my life and I knew my future wouldn't have many as a single mother.

"Does that mean you're saying no to marrying me? Because I'm kind of hoping you are."

"Because it was just a token offer?"

"No," he leaned in, trapping me between his arms and his chest. "Because I'll enjoy convincing you to say yes." He pushed back and helped me off the bed in a rare show of tenderness that he ruined by smacking my ass. "If you get ready in under ten, I might not bitch about the amount of vegetables on your plate."

"Might? I accept that challenge." With a smile unlike any I'd felt in a long time, I went to freshen up and change.

For a dinner date.

With my one-night stand and future baby daddy.

# Chapter 10

*Lasso*

It turned out that I liked sharing a meal with Rocky, and we were doing it a lot. She was a smartass and funny as hell, but she was smart too. Book and street smart but she didn't rub it in your face like some women did. She just *was*.

"I can't believe you made stir-fry. Who makes stir-fry at home?"

She shrugged, looking adorably rumpled and somehow sexy at the same time in her light green tunic that hid the denim shorts I knew she wore only because I'd caught her bending over earlier. "I like to cook and with the internet you can learn pretty much anything."

"You're good at that, taking a bunch of shitty vegetables and turning them into a delicious meal. Is that ginger?"

Her smile lit her up face when she confirmed there was fresh ginger in the dish. "You have a good palate, and I thought all you ate were military packs and steaks."

I frowned, and she rolled her eyes.

"Because you're from Texas."

I smiled and shook my head. "I did my time eating MRE's. They're not as bad as you think but they're also not this damn good."

I knew if I let her, we'd continue to have these meals and we'd shoot the shit, talking about our likes and dislikes, favorite musicians and movies. Even though we'd gone out a few times, it was like a first date, getting to know each other, but it was still surface bullshit. If we were going to have a kid and if I had a chance of convincing Rocky to marry me, we had to dig deeper. "Who taught you how to cook?"

"The internet," she said drily, her eyes blank and shoulders stiff. "Dad wasn't around much so it was up to me to look after myself. After a while bologna sandwiches got old and then I discovered the Food Network. From there the world was my oyster."

"Shit, I thought my hovering parents were bad." They were overbearing, and the weight of their expectations could be crushing but we always had the basics. Always.

She moved around the kitchen adding stuff, stirring, tasting while she talked. "Dad wasn't bad, not really, but he didn't have a traditional line of work, which meant he didn't keep a normal schedule. After a job, depending on how it went, he'd have to lay low in whatever city he was in until things cooled down. I was on my own a lot, but I coped."

Rocky was a survivor. No matter what life threw her way, she found a way to make it work for her. It was an admirable trait, one I hoped she'd pass on to our kid.

"My parents," I said, trying to snatch a sample out of the pan before she smacked my hand, "were there with a capital T. Rose Petal, Texas was named after my great-great-great grandmother's English rose skin."

"Whoa."

Big green eyes widened, at the grandeur, the ridiculousness or the pretentiousness of all, I didn't know.

"Right? Anyway, that meant everything was all about appearances. My folks thought they'd dictate my entire life by dangling a sprawling ranch and a big ass trust fund in front of me. They wanted to pick my major in college, the girl I'd marry and what I would do on the ranch until it was time for me to take over, which would have been whenever the hell my daddy felt I was ready."

I smacked the table, the tension of reliving those times enough to make my anger rise.

"So, you joined the military instead and when you came back ran away from all of their expectations? Cool, how does it feel?"

I expected her to tell me family was important and that I needed to reach out to them. That was what everyone had always said, as if it was so fucking tragic that my perfect parents now only had my younger siblings to weigh down with their old school ideas.

"Honestly? It feels damn good."

"Amen to that." She lifted her cup of iced tea and knocked it against my beer bottle with a smile. "Freedom. Ain't nothin' like it."

"You ever been in love?"

"Nope." She shook her head for emphasis and her red hair bounced around her shoulders. "You?"

"Nah. I'm not sure if I believe in it."

She barked out a laugh, clutching her side. "A man who doesn't believe in love, how original." Then she served up the best-tasting veggies I'd had maybe ever.

"Come on now, darlin'," I said, digging in and savoring the ginger. "It's nothing like that. My mama and daddy are in love with each other, as much as either of them can be when they're more concerned with keeping up appearances. Daddy's had a few affairs but as long as no one knows about it, she's all right with it."

"Damn. I don't know if that's tough or stupid," she said. "I mean you're obviously rich since you're throwing out words like trust fund, but aren't affairs like chess pieces for divorce court?"

Some old memories flashed on the screen in my mind but I quickly let them go. "And become a divorcee? Mama would never allow the scandal. Anyway, I think she had her fun, too, but I'd prefer not to think of either of them as sexual beings."

Her laughter was musical as she pushed her plate away and leaned back in her chair. "Your mom sounds hardcore, but I'll bet she's so proud of you."

"She'd be prouder if I came back to Texas to take over the company." Which I would never do. Ever.

"Will you do that eventually?"

"Hell no. Daddy'll run the company until the wake starts, which means I would have wasted my youth working myself into an early grave for a company that wouldn't be mine until he's dead and buried."

## Wonderfully Wrecked

"Wow. Your family is way different than mine. How are your folks going to feel about this whole baby out of wedlock thing?"

"They'll hate it, but they hate everything. But they'll be happy about the baby part."

"Because, lineage, of course."

"Of course," I shot back with a smile and our gazes collided in a long, intense lock that heated the room to boiling. It had been too long since I last slid into her tight little pussy, too long since she clenched around my cock and just that quickly, all I could think about was Rocky.

Naked.

Writhing.

Crying out my name.

"Oh boy, that changed fast." She squirmed in her seat and fanned her face with a nervous laugh.

"Too fast?"

"I want to say yes, absolutely," she began with a breathy whisper, "but I don't like to lie to myself."

"Good, because I want you, Rocky. Holding your body against me every fucking night, feeling the way your nipples harden against my palm. It's good but it's nowhere near enough."

She sucked in a breath and licked her lips and I was gone. On my feet and at her side in just a second. "I need to have you, Rocky."

"I'm right here, Lasso."

Fuck, the way she said my name made my cock bang against my zipper trying to break free of his constraints. One hand cupped the back of her head and my mouth crashed against hers in a feverish kiss. Her lips were soft, her tongue tasted of ginger and garlic and I devoured her. Plunged deep into her mouth and let my tongue explore like it was the first fucking time I'd been there.

She moaned and clung to me, flinging her arms over my shoulders and playing her fingers through my

## Wonderfully Wrecked

hair. Soft hands combined with her soft, lush body and I wasn't sure I'd be able to hang on for much longer. When her other hand slid under my shirt, my muscles twitched and she giggled. "Your body is insane."

I laughed. "Pretty sure that's my line, sweetheart." Her laugh turned to a moan as I cupped my hand between her legs. "Are you ready for me?" She nodded and pushed the t-shirt up my chest and over my head.

"I'm ready. So ready," she growled and flicked a tongue over one nipple and then the other. "So. Fucking. Ready." Her tongue played from nipple to nipple and down my chest, licking and kissing every inch of my chest while she unfastened my pants.

"Rocky," I growled.

"Lasso," she shot back. "Rope me, cowboy."

I did as any good cowboy would, exactly what the lady asked. She shoved my pants down my legs and pushed me into her seat, my hands never leaving her hips, pulling her closer until she stood between my legs, fingertips grazing my hard cock. "Rocky."

"Yes?"

"Suck me or fuck me, but please stop fucking teasing me." And to my fucking delight, she dropped down between my legs and fisted my cock in her hand, looking at it in wonder, like she couldn't believe this was happening. I knew how she felt. Women usually gave blow jobs because they wanted something but when Rocky's soft lips wrapped around my cock and began that slow, moist drag up and down the length, I let out sounds I didn't even know I could make. "Ah, Rocky."

She moaned her response and I could feel her smile as she worked my cock, hands and mouth in unison to drive me insane. Her moans came faster and deeper, like she was enjoying giving me head, taking more of me in like she couldn't get enough of my dick in her mouth.

And then I couldn't think about anything but the soft rasp of her tongue against my even harder than before cock, the way my tip hit the back of her throat, the way her hands gripped my thighs and her throat tightened and swallowed as my orgasm shot out of me, hot jets of come shooting down her throat. "Ah, Rocky, fuck! Yeah! Fuck, yeah!" My hips jerked, and she took me all the way back until her tongue brushed against my balls. "Rocky!"

I lifted her up off the floor and stripped her down, letting my gaze feast on her naked body. Her tits were fuller, but her belly was still mostly flat though I could see a few changes and I fucking liked them. Knowing my baby was inside her, I had to get my mouth on her. "You don't need to, Dallas."

"I know but I need to." Her gaze darkened with desire but her pussy clenched with how bad she wanted me. I lifted her feet and put one on each arm of the chair so she was open to me, pink and wet and slick. I held her open and licked her from her asshole to her clit, letting the low wail of pleasure wash over me.

"Oh!"

Yeah, that was the sound I wanted to hear so I did it again. And again. She was frantic, panting and wiggling while I licked and sucked her little nub and made her cry out sweet nothings, incoherent words of pleasure that made me ache for her.

"Lasso!" Over and over she moaned my name and then her body jerked and my tongue slipped to her back door, drawing another loud gasp from her.

"I see you like that," I told her and did it again. Some women didn't like ass play but most only pretended not to. I was glad Rocky was open so I slipped a finger into her soaking wet pussy and pulled it out slowly, making sure it was coated as I eased the tip into her tight, heart-shaped ass. "Just tell me what you feel."

"Full," she panted. "And good."

My tongue flicked over her clit, over and over until she was writhing and no longer worried about feeling full, instead she squirmed and inched closer. I ate her pussy until her juices coated my face and dripped down my chin, and my finger drilled her tight ass until a powerful orgasm shot out of her.

"Oh, oh Lasso…fuuuuck!"

The picture of her coming apart, flaming curls making her look like some sexy otherworldly creature. Her skin flushed pink and shook with the aftershocks of her orgasm.

Almost made me come again.

"Lasso, wow!"

I chuckled and sat back on the chair, feeling masculine pride when she slid from the table on wobbly legs and straddled my hips.

"Wow is my specialty, darlin'. I can't seem to stop until I've made you scream."

She gripped my cock and lowered herself on to me with a moan that made me so hard my vision blurred.

"I admire that level of dedication," she told me with a little rock of her hips. "And I feel a scream already starting deep inside me."

My hands went to her hips, grabbing her hard enough to bruise as I thrusted up into her. "That deep?"

The little minx grinned and tilted her head back. "Deeper."

I went deeper and harder, faster and harder, slamming into her with all that I had, her sexy gasps of pleasure egged me on, daring me to give her everything.

And I did.

By the time we made our way to the bed in a sweaty heap of limbs, I'd given her everything and then some while she gave back just the same.

Leaving me spent yet eager for another round.

\*\*\*

"Answer your damn phone, Lasso!"

Rocky's sleepy, irritated voice penetrated the fog of sleep but not enough for me to move. When she shoved me, though, I heard the chime of the phone. "Not my phone. Yours," I grunted.

"Mine is on vibrate 'cause I'm not an animal," she groaned and pushed at my shoulders until I sat up and laughed when her phone began to shudder on the nightstand. "Wrong again."

She groaned and sat up, reaching over to flip on a light. Her expression annoyed, then worried. "Why are all the phones ringing?"

That was a good damn question. "Must be an emergency with the club." That was likely enough to have me off the bed and in search of my own damn phone as the symphony of sounds continued.

"None of your club people would be calling me, Dallas."

Her use of my given name brought me up short. "You're right. Answer yours," I told her and sat on the bed beside her as she slid the green button on her screen.

"Hello?" She strained to hear but there was nothing but white noise on the other end. "Hello?" Ten seconds later she ended the call and looked to me. "Now you."

My phone still sat in the kitchen along with the dishes we'd discarded in passion.

"Yeah?" I said, breathless from the rush through the house to catch it before the last ring.

Someone was there but the fucker wasn't speaking, and I knew who it was.

"Fucker." I ended the call and glared at the still ringing phone.

"It was silent," I told Rocky as she joined me in the kitchen, looking better than I ever could in my own damn t-shirt.

She took a deep breath as she stood by the cordless phone fixed to the wall between the kitchen and the dining room, put her hand on the receiver and lifted it from the cradle. "Hello?"

"You can't fucking run from me, Rochelle!" Even across the room I could hear the crazed voice with the maniacal laugh. "I'll find you, bitch!" With a loud *click*, the call was over.

Rocky's face went white and she shook like a leaf in the wind, the phone still in her hand as reality settled over her. "He found me. He found me." She kept repeating the words over and over, scaring the shit out of me.

"It's okay, Rocky. I've got you." My arms went around her, pulling her to my chest while she continued her chant.

"He found me." She pulled back, green eyes slaying me with fear and worry, defeat swimming in her gaze. "I was supposed to be long gone by now, dammit. Now he's found me, and you too."

"Don't worry about me, Rocky. I can take care of myself."

"I know that, you idiot. That doesn't mean you deserve this particular brand of crazy." One hand cupped the side of my jaw and she smiled wistfully. "I'm sorry about all this."

"Me too."

"If I leave within the hour, I can put a few states between me and them, but you should probably call your club. You're going to need them."

Rocky was pissing me off and she was so busy making plans that she didn't even realize it. I followed her down the hall and back to our room. "Where the fuck do you think you're going?"

She turned with a frown. "I have to get out of here, Lasso."

"I thought you were going to let me take care of you. Or was that just bullshit for a few more nights of fucking?"

She laughed but it was harsh and cold and bitter. "No dick is worth risking my life, Lasso. Not even yours."

"Then, what the fuck?"

She sighed like I was the crazy one. "I heard you talking to your club friend. They don't want this trouble any more than I do. I understand that, but now Genesis is coming after you, too, and they'll be ready to fight for you. Me? Not so much."

"And what about you?"

Her smile was sad when she told me, "I can take care of myself."

"I know you can, but you don't have to. I'm here, I'm a badass and I am your personal fucking protection." She laughed and buried her face in my chest.

"You might be a badass, but we're compromised."

She was right about that and I didn't know whether to kiss her, fuck her or marry her. It was the middle of the night, a stone's throw from Vegas, and I could do all three before the sun came up.

KB Winters

# Chapter 11

*Rocky*

"We talked about this. It's important that you keep your stress to a minimum, Rochelle." Dr. Tipton gave me her best chastising smile as she took her seat beside the exam table.

"I'm working on it, Doc. But sometimes life conspires against me and it's happening with alarming frequency these days." It was the truth, but I knew she was right. I couldn't let the stress get the better of me. "I'm open to suggestions."

"Yoga. Some facilities even offer prenatal yoga, but the most important thing of all is to make sure you're handling it in a healthy way."

"Like sex?" The doctor smirked but I was sure she heard that question all the time. "That's a good stress reliever, isn't it?"

"It is," she said, and I could hear Lasso chuckling in the chair next to her. "And it is a perfectly acceptable method of stress relief, provided you're safe and you don't ignore signs of pain or discomfort." She stared at her chart before turning back to me. "How's your nausea?"

"Still here."

She nodded and looked down again. "You haven't gained as much weight as you should, but your weight isn't concerning. Yet."

"Shouldn't she have a bigger belly already?" Lasso had finally risen from the dead and asked a question since he'd demanded that I let him drive me to the appointment and then he just wormed his way into the exam room using the worried first-time dad routine. It worked like a charm.

"It's also fine. One day you both will wake up and you'll find it there. Don't worry unless there's something to worry about." With a kind smile, Dr. Tipton washed her hands and prepared to let me hear my baby's heartbeat for the very first time. "Ready?"

I gave a sharp nod. "And terrified. Is that normal?"

"It's perfectly normal, Rochelle. Now, listen."

I closed my eyes as the room filled with a steady *thump-thump-thump* in rapid succession, over and over again. *Thump-thump-thump.* "That's...the most beautiful thing I've ever heard in my short, miserable life."

"Incredible," Lasso whispered, and I opened my eyes to find him standing above me, one hand resting on my shoulder in a proprietary manner. Like I was his and he was mine.

"Yeah, it's incredible. It's not too fast is it? Or too slow? Which is worse, fast or slow?" My head was spinning with a thousand questions, more pressing than ever, now that my kid's heartbeat was the soundtrack to my mental processes.

"Baby's healthy. As it should be."

With my nerves settled, I cleaned up and redressed, making an appointment for the next month before Lasso escorted me out of the hospital with one hot hand on my lower back. "That was amazing. My baby's heartbeat."

"*Our* baby's heartbeat. It's my baby too."

I sighed and accepted his help getting into the SUV. "I'm not trying to take away your role in all this, Lasso. But you never said you wanted to be involved and I can't afford to wait until you decide."

"You're kidding right?" He shifted the gear back to Park and turned to me. "I asked you to marry me at least fifteen times and you still haven't given me an answer."

"You don't love me!"

"And you don't love me, so fucking what? We're having a baby."

He just didn't get it.

"We all didn't have the luxury of a loving home and an idyllic childhood, Lasso. You walked away from yours for good reasons but I'd like a chance to have that for myself and for my kid."

## Wonderfully Wrecked

It wasn't something I'd ever admitted out loud—ever—because it was *my* dream, just for *me*. If it didn't work out, no one would ever know.

"And you think I can't give you that?"

"I think that without love, the hard shit is that much harder to deal with. When you're around out of obligation, it's easier to book it when life gets too life-y."

"So, you want love even if it kills our baby?"

"If the baby's dead, I'm dead. Remember?" I turned away from him. "I'm not having this conversation. Let's go."

He put the car in Drive, fuming as he turned out of the parking lot. He was a man not used to feeling helpless and I knew it had to eat him up inside, but this was my life. I couldn't let him just start running it now. He would never stop, and I'd never be able to take care of myself again.

"I'm not trying to be an asshole, Rocky."

"I know, but you are trying to get me to make decisions about my life that I'm not ready to make. I know Genesis is nuts and that can be dangerous, and I've seen his goons' work, so I know what I'm up against. But I can't—no I won't—compromise myself just to make you feel better."

"That's not what I'm asking."

"Isn't it?"

"No," he sighed and looked in his rearview mirror for at least the tenth time since we started driving. "I'm so fucking worried, Rocky. All the damn time, do you get that? I don't usually worry about anything, so this has kind of fucked me up, okay?"

"Was that so hard? I mean I know you guys live and die by the idea that you're so frustratingly emotionally constipated that nothing real ever gets discussed."

"Quiet," he growled.

"Don't tell me to be quiet, dammit! Just listen one damn minute."

## Wonderfully Wrecked

"Rocky, shut up!"

My mouth snapped shut and I stared at him.

"That car has been following us since we left the hospital. Does it look familiar?"

I turned over my shoulder to see what had spooked the big bad Lasso. A shiver went down my spine when I saw the yellow Trans Am with a black dragon on the front hood. I knew it well.

"That's Big Boy's pride and joy."

"Good to know," he grunted and hit a sharp right and then another before losing our inconspicuous tail.

"Now darlin', we plan."

## Chapter 12

*Lasso*

The yellow fucking Trans Am was still on our ass, following every turn and attempt at misdirection. Who in the hell used a neon yellow sports car to trail someone? I wasn't complaining because it made the asshole easier to spot, but it also meant being invisible wasn't his priority.

"We can't go back to your place," Rocky said. "If they found us they probably followed us from there." Her voice was cold and blank, like she was in shock, only used to it. "We need to lose them."

I frowned and looked at the cool-headed creature beside him. "Them? Do you know who's with him?" I couldn't see who was in the car because I wouldn't let them get close enough for that shit.

"No, but I'm sure I can guess. Probably Mosko or Guerilla. They're both crazy as hell and if they're not dead, that's who he'd send."

Her gaze kept flicking to the side mirror every few seconds, giving away the nerves she did a damn good job of hiding.

"Shit. I would've liked more time to plan this out but—"

She glanced around and barked, "But that's not the story of my life. Look, we have to get rid of them and then we can figure out what to do."

Before she picked up her phone and started typing, she checked the windows. "Okay, get on the freeway in half a mile and then stay in the left lane until I say otherwise."

I frowned at her cool, bossy tone. "I think we should—"

"Just fucking listen to me for now. I've got this, yeah?"

I nodded at her confidence and pulled behind a moving van to turn onto the freeway.

I had no idea what was going through her pretty little head, but I merged into the lane and punched the

## Wonderfully Wrecked

gas until I was in the left lane going about ten miles over the speed limit and climbing.

"Want to fill me in?" I asked, moving the car forward as I spotted the yellow eyesore swerving through traffic to catch up with us. "Big Boy's closing in."

Rocky didn't even look up, she just nodded and slid her finger over the phone screen. "I know. He'll keep two cars between us," she said absently, looking up at the sign we passed and back to her phone. "As soon as we pass the next overhead sign, get in the middle lane and do it quickly. Speed up and then hit the brakes before you get over."

I laughed. "Rocky, I think I know how to—"

"Now!"

I did what she said, watching in the rearview mirror as the Trans Am scrambled to get over and having trouble with the thick crush of cars as we drew closer to the heart of Las Vegas. "Seriously?"

She nodded and looked up at me before casting a quick glance over her shoulder. "Pay attention Lasso, we need to do it again."

"Where are we going?"

"The strip. Do you have anyone who can leave us a different *nondescript* car somewhere?"

"Yeah." I handed her my phone. "Dial Savior and put it on speakerphone." She did what I said, barely sparing me a glance, which I should have been relieved about because this would have been a complete fucking nightmare if she panicked. Instead *she* was saving *us*. "I need you to leave me the blue sedan," I began.

"At the Bellagio parking garage," Rocky called out.

"You heard that?"

"Yeah. What's up?" Savior's voice was gruff and annoyed, probably because I interrupted something with him and Mandy.

"Can't talk now. I'll explain later but if you can do that ASAP we'd really fucking appreciate it."

He groaned again. "Shit yeah. I'll leave a little something for you in there," he said and clicked off.

I opened my mouth to tell Rocky she could drop the phone, but she spoke first. "Okay we have a mile to go so listen."

"I know how to get to the Bellagio," I told her, only mildly impatient.

Rocky let out an annoyed sigh of her own. "The car isn't there yet and I know how to get there, too. Speed up and find a space to get in that's just big enough for one car. One car, Lasso. And keep your turn signal on."

I smiled. "This bossy side of you is really fucking hot, Rocky. I just wanted you to know."

Her cheeks stained a sexy shade of pink and I laughed.

"Yeah, thanks."

She shook her head, eyes going to the yellow car trying desperately to catch up with us.

"Take this exit at the last possible minute even if you have to cut someone off."

"Ooh, a bad girl."

Watching her turn out so capable and direct, so focused on her goal, was hot as fuck. I followed her instructions just like it had been drilled in me to do on the ranch as a kid and then the military as a man, cutting off a cube truck and blocking our exit from Big Boy and his companion.

"Excellent." She beamed a smile up at me and placed a hand on my forearm as we took the curve that would get us closer to The Strip. "Now we just have to get lost in this traffic until your friend can get us the new car."

"So, this is what you do? Figure out how to win in any given situation?"

She shrugged like it was no big deal, but I was damned impressed and more determined than ever to keep her safe because now I knew just how far Genesis would go to keep her.

"No, I plan shit and I do it well."

"Yeah, I can see that."

If this was how she worked on the fly, I could only imagine the kind of money Genesis and his guys had pulled in.

"Let's keep your skills between us for now, okay?"

She nodded. "Fine by me. Turn into this parking garage," she said, still focused on her phone.

"This isn't where we're going."

"I know that, Lasso," she said, words dripping with annoyance. "Just turn, please."

I maneuvered into the right lane and turned into the parking garage and grabbed a ticket. "We don't want them to spot us, not even from far away. Take the south exit out of here."

That's what we did for what felt like an hour, drive in and out of parking garages until we got word from Savior. "You plan on running from them forever?"

"No, Lasso, I don't." She set her phone in her lap and held mine, eagerly awaiting the call. "Right now, my goal is to stay alive."

Right. We both jumped when the ringing phone broke the silence in the car and she hit the answer button.

"Savior."

"Sixth floor right by the ramp. Six four nine." He disconnected the call and my shoulders relaxed. I'd feel better if we could get inside, at least for a little while. Rocky guided me through another garage that led us to Las Vegas Boulevard and to our final destination.

We quickly switched cars, leaving the ticket under the windshield of mine for whichever of the prospects were assigned to retrieve it.

"This is a good choice," she commented as she slid into the passenger seat. "We should swing by your place first."

## Wonderfully Wrecked

Was this the pregnancy brain everyone was talking about? "Didn't you just say the house was probably compromised?"

She shrugged. "I said *swing by*. If they know where you live that's where they'll be waiting for us to return since they were dumb enough to lose us on the road."

Shit, she made a good point. "Fine." I turned back out of the parking spot and we took the long route home just in case.

When I pulled into the driveway Rocky grinned. "At least we have one more night of normalcy."

I let out a frustrated groan as I stepped from the car. How in the hell were we going to survive this? Without my brothers, we were doubly fucked.

\*\*\*

"Your focus is for shit this week man, what's up?" Golden Boy had done what he needed to. After two days of half-assing my job he called me to his office.

"Just some shit going on that I need to deal with." I hadn't returned any of Savior's calls since he dropped off the car and I knew he had questions, but I wasn't ready. Rocky claimed she was working on an exit plan, but she was so fucking tight-lipped I didn't know if that was bullshit or not.

"Tell me about it."

I looked at Golden Boy with his long fucking mane of blond hair. The contented look he wore was so different from the man who'd returned to us after six years of wrongful incarceration. He was relaxed and happy. That caged animal look was gone. And I thought maybe if anyone would understand, it would be him. "Has anyone told you anything about Rocky?"

"The chick you banged at Max's wedding who showed up claiming to be pregnant with your kid? Maybe a little," he smirked.

"That smartass girlfriend of yours is rubbing off on you."

"Plenty of rubbing does go on," he said with a dirty grin and I rolled my eyes. "And she's my fiancée now, asshole."

I guess I'd been more absent than I realized. "I hadn't heard. Congratulations. It's about time. I was wondering how many kids you'd have before you married the woman, shit."

"Please. Teddy has put it off so much I'm beginning to get a complex about it." His wide, shit-eating grin made a liar out of him. "She has her reasons and I respected them, then one day out of the blue she stands in front of me naked as the day she was born and says, 'I'm ready to marry you.'" He shook his head, his expression pure disbelief even now. "That was it and here we are."

"I'm happy for you, Golden Boy. If anyone deserves all this, it's you."

"You too, it looks like." His expression was now serious, something it was still hard to get used to after months of scowling and angry absence. "There is nothing on the fucking planet that would ever stand between me and my family. Nothing and no one could stop me from doing what I could to protect them. Not the law and not the club," he said pointedly, and I knew he'd been looped in on our earlier discussions. "Family is family, Lasso. No matter what kind of family it is, no one knows that shit more than guys like us. But sometimes, a man has to do what the fuck he has to do. Know what I'm sayin'?"

I nodded because I knew exactly what he was saying. No matter how it happened between us, Rocky was mine to protect. She'd scoff at me saying it like that, but it was true. Our child was growing inside her and I had to keep them both safe. Whether the Reckless Bastards had my six or not. "Thanks, Golden Boy."

"Anytime. But before you do anything stupid, talk to Cross again."

I grunted yes because that was what he wanted to hear but nothing had changed in that regard.

"I can handle it but thanks."

I spent the rest of the shift coming up with different plans that didn't involve running away even though I knew that was what Rocky wanted. We were safer here in Mayhem with the MC than on the road in unfamiliar surroundings. Things had gone quiet for the past two days, but they wouldn't stay that way forever.

"Come on Lasso, lets close up shop and grab a beer." Jag stood at the entryway to my station where I was putting away the tattoo gun and straightening my shit, so I wouldn't have to do it tomorrow.

"Can't. Got some shit to take care of tonight."

"One drink," Jag insisted, sounding impatient. "Come on."

I followed Jag out and we made the short drive to the clubhouse. Instead of going inside where it sounded like there was a party going on, we grabbed a six pack from the fridge in the back and sat outside. The clubhouse was far enough away from Vegas that the lights were a sight rather than a nuisance. We could see occasional stars in the sky, burning bright on a clear night like this. "What's up, Jag?"

"That was going to be my line. You're quiet as fuck, you don't talk to anyone and I haven't seen you in days. What's going on?"

I took a long pull on the dark beer, letting the bitter icy liquid slide down my throat. "Nothing. I've just been busy."

"And Rocky? How is she?"

I sighed and looked at Jag. He was my closest friend but right now I couldn't separate that from the club's refusal to help and that wasn't fair to him. "She's fine. Still sick on and off all day and so fucking emotional. She cried when an old man was found guilty on Law & Order and wanted to throw away the TV after watching cable news for three hours. Straight."

Jag whistled, looking equally horrified and amused. "You don't look like you hate it."

## Wonderfully Wrecked

"I don't," I admitted to him and myself for the first time. "She's stubborn and barely lets me help with anything but I don't hate it." I should. A baby was not in my plans right now but there was one on the way and I wanted it. I wanted Rocky, too, but that would have to wait until she was out of harm's way.

"Let me know if I can do anything, Lasso. I know you're not happy with...shit but you know I got your back. Shit, you do know that right, asshole?"

I laughed, and we knocked our beer bottles together. "Yeah, I know it and I appreciate it, dickhead." It was good to know that if the time came where I needed help, I would have some. "What's new with you?"

"Nothing much. You ever think about friends you lost touch with when you went into the service?"

"Sometimes but not much. Most of those guys were hometown boys. After college they'd go back and run the family business and marry a local girl."

Jag laughed. "I always forget you're from Mayberry."

"Rose Petal," I corrected more out of habit than any desire for him to know. The smile died on my face when I saw Cross ambling towards us.

"Cross."

"Lasso. How's it going?"

I shrugged, not really in the mood to talk. This was why I didn't want to come here or go out anywhere. I didn't want to pretend I wasn't pissed the fuck off. "It's going. You?"

Cross shrugged and Jag laughed. "Mighty fine weather we're having folks," he said, his face lighting up at his joke.

Cross and I glared at him and he only laughed harder. "Oh sorry, I thought we were doing bullshit small talk impressions. Hey, I see someone I know over there," he said. "I'm heading home anyway. See you guys later." Then Jag quickly left me alone with the club Prez.

Cross asked, "You gonna run from me forever?"

I stopped and turned to Cross, my hands tingling with the urge to punch him in the fucking face.

"I'm not running, Cross. I just have shit I need to take care of, if that's all right with you?" He nodded and I walked off, making a beeline for my bike before anyone else decided they wanted to fucking chitchat.

"Yo, Lasso! Wait up, man." Savior's gravelly voice grew closer. "What's your hurry?"

"Shit to do." I should have that printed on a t-shirt since it was becoming my mantra.

"Ran into your girl the other day coming from the shooting range. She ran away from me and sped off like I was chasing her."

Of course, Rocky hadn't said one word to me about it until well after the fucking fact. "Yeah she heard our entire conversation and I had to drive to fucking Arizona to track her down."

It wasn't Savior's fault, but I felt good laying the blame on his feet for the club's reluctance to help out a woman in need.

"Oh, shit man, that's rough. Let me know if there's anything I can do."

I gave him a look and he shrugged and said, "That's not up to me."

Bullshit. "I have to go," and turned for the parking lot.

"Lasso don't do this. Not for some chick you don't know."

"You mean like you didn't know Mandy, not since she was a kid. But we all showed up to help keep her safe. I got it. See you around."

This would all blow over. Eventually. Maybe.

I revved up the motorcycle and took off for the open road. The cool evening air washed over my bare forearms, and the exposed skin at the back of my neck. By the time I walked up to my house and stepped inside, I didn't want to punch anyone and when I caught a whiff of Rocky's flowery, earthy scent, punching someone was the last thing on my mind.

She was sprawled out on the sofa in nothing but a pink tank top and a pair of pink panties. *Only* a tank and panties. Large, hard pink nipples winked at me through the thin cotton until my mouth watered. She was a fucking vision lying there asleep and my cock grew hard. Why couldn't I stop wanting her?

It was a question for another time because now, I questioned my sanity when I picked her up and carried her to my bed. It was pure torture, all that silky soft skin and womanly curves pressed up against me, the way she nuzzled into my neck even in her sleep. Oh God, how I wanted to strip her down and drive into her wet, hot pussy, but I couldn't. I put her to bed, showered, and curled my naked body around hers while I drifted off to sleep.

Nothing had ever felt as good as the weight of Rocky's body against mine, until I felt the swell of our baby beneath my hands.

## Chapter 13

*Rocky*

Being out of work was not as liberating as I thought it would be when I was working two jobs and wishing for enough cash to check out completely.

I was bored and climbing the walls. It had been three days since we'd spotted Big Boy's car hawking us and I still didn't have a solid getaway plan. My mind wouldn't stop working trying to come up with something that wouldn't force me to take Lasso's kid away from him but would keep me out of Genesis' reach.

Every plan I came up with had a flaw, so I reverted back to form. Crafts had always helped me in the past, so I bought some nice organic Merino wool and started making a baby blanket. It was three shades of green ranging from shamrock to teal, in a hypnotic swirling pattern. As I settled into a mindless design, it pushed away all the clutter in my mind—Lasso and the baby and my business—so I could find a plan to get me free.

Just because I hadn't seen his fat ass in a few days didn't mean Big Boy had gone back to California. They wouldn't go until I was with them or in the ground, and details started to slide into place. I needed an isolated location that couldn't be linked to me, just enough to send Genesis and his thugs running all over the country for me, exhausting time and resources to find someone they should assume was dead.

I froze at the creak of the back door. Lasso had said he would fix it at least a hundred times this week because the screen door squeaked like crazy. He hadn't gotten to it yet and I didn't hear that deafening bike of his, so I reached behind the sofa for the bat that had been with me since I'd left Florida.

My right hand wrapped around the handle and I pushed up to a standing position, taking slow careful steps toward the kitchen, avoiding the noisy parts of the floor. I turned at the hall and ran smack into Navajo, the blondest white boy I'd ever seen with iceberg blue eyes and a hard on for all things Native American. Or Native American adjacent. His angry scowl resonated first, and I screamed.

"Loud bitch," he grunted and punched me square in the face. His grubby, calloused knuckle hit me square in the nose. The awful crunching noise sounded first and then the feel of warm blood sliding down my nose and over my lips.

"Fucker," I grunted and stumbled back. I bit back a groan when the bat knocked against my ankle and grinned as I pulled my arm back and cracked the bat against his shins.

"You crazy bitch, that's a metal bat!"

"Aluminum, actually. Light weight but hurts like hell."

Navajo rolled around on the kitchen floor between the metal work table and the sink, groaning and gripping his shins. "Just come back with us, Rochelle, make it easy on yourself."

"I can't do that, Navajo. I won't."

"You will. Eventually. You think the Reckless Bastards will fight a war with us over you? You overestimate your importance, sweetheart."

He might have been right about that, but I wasn't counting on some biker gang and I wasn't counting on Lasso either. Not when I wasn't sure that he could be trusted yet.

"Yet here you are, chasing me down. I'm not going back, Navajo and fuck you for thinking any of this is all right." I'd quickly unrolled a yard of paper toweling from holder I'd been able to reach on the counter and jammed it under my nose. It had already filled with blood.

"We all got jobs to do, Rochelle."

He grunted, too much, as he wiggled around before lunging at me, a switchblade clutched in his hands.

"Ow, you crazy bitch!" he said when I whacked him again with the bat. He looked at me with wild blue eyes, clutching his now aching forearm.

## Wonderfully Wrecked

"And we all have to fight for the life we want." I stood and he grabbed my ankle, forcing me to send the handle of the bat flying into his nose in a sudden need for revenge. He dropped like a rock.

I made it to the phone and dialed Lasso. "Trouble at the house. Come quick. And alone." I ended the call and took a seat in a chair at the small table in the corner of the kitchen, keeping a close eye on a now unconscious Navajo while I waited. Head back with fresh paper towels under my nose, tapping my feet, I was the definition of anxious.

I was lucky Navajo had drawn the short straw today. He had more heart than brain and lacked the cruel streak Genesis preferred in his men. It could have been real bad and all I had was a fucking bat, making me really regret not taking Lasso up on his offer to get a gun. Maybe we'd revisit that later. After we dealt with the unconscious gangster on the kitchen floor.

I couldn't believe I was sitting around once again waiting for a man. But this was the kind of shit Lasso wanted me to include him in, so I would.

"What's going on?" He didn't waste any time, pushing inside the house and stalking straight to the kitchen where he was brought up short. "Who the fuck is this?"

"Navajo. Remember him from San Diego? One of Genesis' men you bloodied that night. He's alive. Just had a run in with a bat." Lasso smirked but his face and his body were lined with anxiety. Around his mouth and eyes, pulling his shoulders and spine tight, he was one big ball of tension.

"I remember. What's he doing here?"

I rolled my eyes and sat back down. "I invited him over for tea, thought we could work out some kind of fucking treaty."

"Smartass." Lasso had his phone out and was mumbling into it, calling, I assumed, members of his own gang to come and deal with this shit.

I heard, "Cross, need some help at the house." There were a few more mumbled words and then he shoved the phone into his back pocket.

"It doesn't sound to me like you called the police." Arms crossed, I stared at him, demanding an explanation with my silence.

"The club can handle it."

I could tell by his expression that he believed it, but they were his friends not mine. The Reckless Bastards hadn't earned my loyalty yet.

"No offense but I don't need this *handled* that way. He broke in and I defended myself, end of story."

"The cops will never believe—"

"I'll make them believe it and that's that. Don't even think about going behind my back on this." My biggest fear in all of this was that when the dust settled I'd still be running from Genesis. I couldn't let that happen. No matter what.

"I need you to trust me, to trust *us* on this."

I shook my head, letting him know just how impossible an ask it was.

"I don't. I'm sorry but I don't and I can't afford to. Your friends have made it clear how they feel about helping me and I'm fine with that, but that means I get to decide how I handle the shit that happens to me."

I poked him in his chest just to make sure he got the message.

"Only that baby in your belly means it happens to me too, don't *you* forget that!"

A knock on the door had us both jumping apart and staring as Cross entered the house with who I assumed to be Jag and Savior.

"Are we interrupting?" one of them said.

"Like it matters," I mumbled, bending to pick up my phone and call the police. "Lasso made a mistake calling you, the police will be here soon."

Cross, in a show of power, stared at me and took a seat in the living room while Lasso and his friend followed suit. "We'll wait with you. Just to be safe."

It didn't matter. Not to me anyway. I knew Lasso was pissed about their reluctance to help but it was easier for me on my own. I didn't have to consult anyone else on my plans and I could leave whenever I wanted. Now I had ties, dammit. "Do whatever you want," I shrugged.

***

The phone rang, making me drop a stitch in the new booties I was knitting for the Olympic soccer player growing in my belly, at least that was what he or she was practicing for today. I ignored the phone because I didn't want to talk to anybody.

The ringing stopped for about thirty seconds before it started up again. And again. And again. My patience was so fucking close to snapping that I yanked the phone off the table and answered without looking at the screen. "Yeah?"

"Come home and your boyfriend lives."

Genesis. "Fuck off." I hung up the phone and let out a primal scream that was so filled with pain and frustration there was a good chance it would split me in half. I couldn't let him get to me because that was what he wanted, to get in my head. To make me afraid.

The ringing started up again and I let it ring because I couldn't decide what was the better option, the incessant fucking trill of my old school ringtone or Genesis and his pathetic words. I answered when it rang again because I knew it wouldn't stop, not until he said what he had to say.

"What?"

"Remember when we went to Catalina for the first time? You squealed like a little girl at the glass bottomed boat." This was the *calm before the storm* Genesis, where he pretended everything was all right and that he was a normal sane man.

"I remember." It started out as a great little getaway. "I also remember you losing your shit because a guy offered to buy me a drink. And you ruined the rest of the weekend because you turned into an overly aggressive alpha dick to everyone. Me included."

## Wonderfully Wrecked

He growled until it became an all-out roar. "You always remember the bad shit!"

I laughed. "Because it was all bad shit with you, Genesis. You're unstable and insecure and I'm not interested." Five. Four. Three. Two.

"Then you both will fucking die!" There he was. The unstable asswipe I was used to dealing with. "That's too bad, Rochelle. We could have been good together."

I laughed again and hung up the phone, knowing he would call again. "Hello?" I answered like I didn't know who it might be on the other end of the line.

"Just one job, Rochelle. One fucking job so we can recoup what we lost when one of the stash houses was raided. Fuck!" I'd seen a couple of their stash houses, so I knew he'd lost at least a couple million dollars.

"No. Maybe you should recruit more stable criminals and you wouldn't have drunk assholes running their mouths when they shouldn't." I froze as I finished speaking and I put him on speakerphone, so

I could type something into a notepad. I hoped it wouldn't come to that, but details were currency when you were fighting for your life.

"Maybe you should think about who the fuck you're talking to, Rochelle. Out of respect for our past, I tried to do this the easy way."

I laughed again because I knew it would piss him off. The man couldn't handle being laughed at. "The easy way was sending your goons to fuck up my life and beat up my friends? Good to know."

"You left me!"

"You're a fucking nut job, Genesis, and I'm not coming back. You do what you gotta do and I'll do the same, fuck you very much."

This time I put the phone on silent and sat with my half-finished baby booties in my lap. And then, I cried like the baby I was carrying. Genesis continued to call, as evidenced by the voicemail chime that sounded every couple of minutes. I refused to listen to them.

## Wonderfully Wrecked

That was how Lasso found me when he came home, bawling like a wounded banshee over a damp half of a baby booty.

"What's wrong, Rocky?"

I opened my mouth to speak and a squeak came out, followed by more tears. My shoulders shook, and I was sure my skin was the color of an overripe tomato.

The seat cushions shifted under Lasso's weight and his big, warm arms circled my body and pulled me close. "If you're crying about the lack of tacos in the house, don't. I brought like twenty of 'em from that truck you follow around town."

I smacked his chest. "I follow them on Twitter and then when I'm hungry I go where they are. It's how the food industry works, cowboy."

Every one of my words was still muffled by tears and worry flashed in those big blue eyes of his, so I shoved my phone at him.

"Did you...what the fuck?" He glared at me, angry and worried as Genesis' psychotic ramblings played out in his ear. Lasso cut off the words after a few minutes and turned to me. "Rocky," he said, sounding disappointed and hurt. And pissed off.

"I know what you're going to say. And you're probably right." It wasn't just me involved anymore and I should have told him. "I'm still trying to figure things out and that's all I can say," I told him as my tears finally began to dry.

Blue eyes studied me and then went to my phone and back, like he was trying to figure out some damn riddle.

"You know I'm going to kill that shit stain, don't you?"

I nodded, secretly echoing those sentiments. "I know you want to, but I'm not going to let you."

"Feeling nostalgic and kindhearted towards your ex?"

"Fuck no, I'm feeling like he isn't worth running from a murder charge." It was my turn to take his face in my hands, force his eyes to look in mine so he could see how deadly fucking serious I was about this.

"I don't know you well Lasso, but I do know that you're a good man with a good heart."

"No, I'm not," he insisted, and I only smiled because in my experience, the actual good ones never thought they were.

"And no, you don't know me that well."

"You are, trust me. I also know that I don't know much about your motorcycle gang."

"Club," he corrected.

"Fine, I don't know much about your *club* but I'm guessing that saving my life won't be a good enough excuse for any lawman to shy away from trying to nail a biker gang—er—club. If you really think about it, you know it's true."

He pushed back out of my grasp with a dark frown. "You're seriously worried about this?"

I sighed. "Like it or not Lasso, this baby is yours too. I'm never going to be safe from Genesis, but this baby can be, but only if you're not locked up in some prison."

"I won't make you a promise I'm not sure I can keep, Rocky, but I promise to make sure you and our baby are safe. Always."

I believed him and when he cupped my face and pressed his forehead against mine, I knew we were in this together. I'd have to make sure that if it came down to it, I'd be the one who took Genesis out.

In another life I might have deserved a man like Lasso, even if he was in a biker gang. Excuse me, *motorcycle club*. He was truly a good man and I'd put him in an impossible position and he just went with it. Rolled with it like it was totally fucking natural to be tangled up with a crazy fucker like Genesis.

I rested my forehead on his chest and breathed, "I can live with that. For now."

"Good, because I can't handle your tears."

I lifted my head and rolled my eyes. "Typical male. Wants to go up against a psychopath but you're afraid of a few drops of salty water."

I laughed and when he pulled away, I reached for him, pressing my mouth to his and letting myself get lost in him. In that moment, I could pretend we had the potential to be something more. I could pretend that when his hands went to my hips and pulled me onto his lap, pressing me against his steel hard cock, that we were making love. That we were celebrating something deeper than the basic desire to come.

"Are we doing this?" he growled.

His big hands were on my tits, cupping them while he pinched them between his thumb and forefinger and I arched into him. His mouth dropped to one breast, sucking it through the thin fabric of my t-shirt and I let out a hiss, arching to feed him more of me.

"Seems like we are," I purred. "Is that a problem?"

My hips moved on their own, sliding back and forth along his cock, desire flooding my veins until it was the only thing I could think about.

"Not when you do that," he ground out between clenched teeth.

"What about this?" I grabbed the hem of my tank and pulled it over my head, feeling my nipples harden at his heated gaze. While Lasso stared, I stood and got rid of my shorts and panties, standing there and feeling like a supermodel at the way he was gawking at me.

"I guess I'm on my own," I said playfully, teasing his gaze as I slid one hand down my belly and between my legs, tossing my head back.

"Fucking tease," he growled and got to his feet, scooping me in his arms on his way to the bedroom. I touched myself while he took off his clothes, feeling my fingers get wetter at his inability to look away.

"Rocky."

I smiled and pretended he was mine. "You're too far away."

## Wonderfully Wrecked

With his wild blond hair bouncing as he moved, Lasso knelt on the bed between my thighs and pulled me closer. "Don't worry darlin', we're about to get really close."

And then he was inside me, making me feel good, making me forget the world for a little while.

Making me wish for more.

Making me scream his name until I passed out in his arms.

This had to be the calm before the storm. With my fucking luck, it just had to be.

# Chapter 14

*Lasso*

I used to think waking up next to a woman was a sign of dark things to come, things like commitment and picket fences. But waking up beside Rocky was an experience, always. She was soft and warm, and she smelled so goddamn good I had a hard time tearing myself away from her. But mornings like this, after we spent the whole night wrapped up in each other, I woke up with a big shit eating grin on my face.

Rocky's face was buried in the crook of my neck, her lips and tongue sliding against my skin as one hand slid up and down my chest. One hand instantly went to her ass and pulled her flush against me. "Good morning."

The purr of her voice vibrated against my skin and set my nerve endings on edge and when she kicked her leg over me to straddle my hips, my cock grew even harder. "Good morning to you too."

"Shaping up to be," she shot back with a smile in her voice, hips grinding on me in a hypnotic circular motion that had me on the verge of snapping. Her pussy slid across my cock, sliding around my balls and I groaned.

"You didn't get enough last night?"

"I didn't," she purred and sat up as the tip of my cock breached her slick opening. "But I'm eager to find out how much is enough."

I gripped her hips as she slid down my cock, up and down in a quick dragging motion that had me breaking out in a sweat. Her heavy tits hung in perfect teardrops, her belly slightly protruded as she rode my cock. I wanted to thrust into her, but I was too mesmerized by watching her hips grind, her head fall back in pleasure to do anything more than enjoy.

"Do you smell that?" I frowned as a hint of smoke touched my nostrils but Rocky continued to ride me.

"No. Yes." She froze and looked me. "Shit, yeah. Smoke."

## Wonderfully Wrecked

She didn't breathe for a moment and then she was off me in a flash, giving no thought to the precarious position we'd just been in. "Why do I smell smoke?"

While she paced the room naked, I slipped on a pair of jeans from the floor and placed my hands on her shoulders to stop her pacing. I made sure she looked in my eyes until she was calm.

"Quiet. I'll go check things out, stay here."

"I'll call 911."

"Not this time, sweetheart." I kissed her forehead and grabbed my piece. "I'll let you know if I need the cops but maybe put some clothes on?"

"Bananas. Say bananas if you need help. I'll call the cops and come get your six," she said confidently.

My eyes went wide, and I smiled. "My six? How do you know about six?"

"I know it's military for I got your back, cowboy. I know a lotta things you don't know."

"Good to know," I told her and slipped out, on alert as the smell of smoke grew stronger. At the end of the hall I spotted the source of the smell, a burning potato chip bag in the ashtray on the coffee table. And on my sofa sat a big ass black man with a bald head. He was at least three hundred pounds and wider than my stainless still fridge.

He heard me coming and tossed some words over his shoulder. "Damn man, I was wondering how many of these fuckers I'd have to burn before you lovebirds smelled it." The psychopath laughed like this was a normal everyday fucking occurrence and held up a paper bag filled with bags of potato chips.

"Big Boy." The other goon I had decked in San Diego when he tried to strong arm Rocky. "You don't write, you don't call . . ."

He nodded, smiling up at me as he swiveled his head on that massive neck.

"You got one minute to tell me why you're in my fucking house before I put a bullet in your mother fucking head." I braced myself for him to try and fight me or take my gun.

Instead the fucker put his hands up and grinned. "Boss is willing to take Rochelle for a few weeks while she plans a job for him and then you can have her back."

"That's not gonna happen, and I think you know that."

He shrugged as I came around the sofa to see his face and more importantly, his hands. He was as ugly in broad daylight as he'd been in the club.

"I figured as much but that was the message, a short exchange. But if that's not agreeable to you, then it's war and I know your crew ain't going to war over no piece of ass. No matter how hot she is."

Smug bastard flashed a smile like he'd been privy to club business.

"There are things you don't know, Big Boy. Things your boss doesn't know either."

I didn't want to tell more people than I needed to about Rocky's pregnancy, but I needed this asshole to know how serious this was.

"Yeah, like what things?"

"Like the fact that Rocky and I have been seeing each other since we ran into you that night."

"Bullshit. We've been down there since then and you haven't been there and she hasn't been here."

"You know, Rocky is a stubborn woman. I should be thanking you guys for finally getting her to move in with me. I asked and asked but she said it was too soon until you goons scared her into my arms. Thanks for that by the way."

Big Boy wasn't so jovial anymore and that wide toothpaste smile was a little dimmer.

"She's worth going to war over?"

"Fuck yeah, she is. So is our baby."

## Wonderfully Wrecked

He blinked as my words sank in. "Fuck, man. Boss is gonna flip his shit when he finds out. Fuck, fuck, fuck. This ain't good, man."

Well that answered my question. It would only make things worse. "Sorry about that, Big Boy."

"Yeah, me too." He moved to stand but I was lighter and faster, and at his side before he could get to his feet.

"Not yet." The butt of my gun crashed down on his jaw and he was out cold. It would be at least an hour before he came to and by then he'd be somewhere where we could get some information out of him.

"Rocky, you dressed?"

The door opened a second later and the floor squeaked. "Is he dead?"

"No, he's out, though. Bring my phone."

"Phone, right," she whispered, and I listened to the shuffle of her feet as she headed back into the bedroom. When she appeared, she was fully dressed but her hair was still rumpled like she just got fucked.

"Phone," she said and handed it to me, flashing a quick look at big boy on the sofa.

I sped dialed the number I needed; it answered in a beat. "My house. Bring the guys."

I shoved the phone in my back pocket, Rocky standing two feet away, shaking like a leaf and nibbling that bottom lip.

"Hey, Rocky. Look at me. Look at me." Her green eyes locked on mine. "Calm down, it's okay. Big Boy is fine, he'll have a massive headache but otherwise he'll be all right." *Maybe.*

"I don't care about Big Boy," she said when she came back down to earth. "It's just, this shit just got super real. Your boys are coming to get him and then what?"

"Are we doing this, Rocky? Complete and total honesty?"

She paused a breath and then nodded. "Yes. Yep."

"They'll take him someplace and keep him there for a while, see what kind of information they can get out of him."

"Why not kill him?"

"Do you want him dead?"

"No, I was just curious."

Time for honesty. "I told him you were pregnant, and I hoped it would change his mind, but he made it clear that it wouldn't. If we don't have to off the motherfucker, we won't. But only time will tell."

She nodded and tucked a few strands of her hair behind her ear. Something was on her mind but I didn't make a big deal about it even though we just agreed no more secrets. "You're right, Lasso. Let's do this. Let's get married."

I opened my mouth to say something and froze. "What?"

"You're right. Let's get married."

She was saying what I wanted to hear but it was off. "Cut the shit, Rocky. What's going on?"

"If something happens to me, anything at all, you can speak for me. If it comes down to it, save the baby first. They won't listen to anyone but family, so we should do it soon." I didn't know how she was being so calm about this, about these kinds of choices. Serious fucking choices.

"Okay?"

I blinked, and her face came back in focus. "I knew you wanted to marry me." I winked and she laughed, smacking my chest as she pushed me away.

"Don't think this means I'm going to be cooking dinner and sucking you off on demand."

She was hot when she was feisty, all fired up and ready to tell me how things would be in our marriage.

"On request is good enough, sweetheart." She smacked my belly again, but her hand slid down my abs and my hand went to her belly and my lips went to hers. The kiss was sweet at first, like new lovers but it quickly heated up and hands began to roam as our passion grew. The heat swirled between us and threatened to spiral out of control.

A knock sounded at the door. "Fuck off!" I yelled at the door and Rocky laughed.

KB Winters

## Chapter 15

*Rocky*

There were at least a dozen bikers in Lasso's living room and I was hiding out in the kitchen, brewing coffee. Like the good little fucking lady. It pissed me off how easily I fell into that role. Fuck that nonsense, I should be out there. It was my life they were discussing and I knew more about Genesis than any of them. But, my dad raised me right even if he did leave me with questionable life skills, so I pulled out some beers and chips and set them on the table while the coffee brewed.

"We have to be sure."

I didn't know who the guy was who said it, but now wasn't the time for niceties.

"Sure, about what?" I asked.

I had a sneaking suspicion I knew what they needed to know. If I had a snowball's chance in hell of surviving this mess with Genesis I'd have to trust these men and that meant we had to be open.

"You want to be sure this baby is Lasso's before you can decide to help me?"

Lasso jumped up, ready to defend my honor but I held up a hand to stop him. Another man with dark hair and dimples stood beside him, Cross, I assumed. "We don't mean no disrespect, Rocky."

And I didn't need his fucking explanation. "I don't care what you did or didn't mean. What I need to know is if the paternity of this child is the deciding factor in getting your help?"

There was no point plotting and planning if they needed hard proof and I looked around at each of the men, some I knew, most I didn't.

"Can you blame us?" Savior, the one who really didn't like me asked the question with such venom, I thought I'd be safer on my own.

"No, I don't. I'm not interested in blame, I just need someone to answer my fucking question."

Their silence said it all.

I was on my own.

"Okay, good to know. I'm not taking any tests until after the baby is born so thanks for your offer, but I'm good on my own."

Cross took a step forward and folded his arms over his chest. "No offense Rocky, but this isn't really up to you."

"Wrong. It's my life and I'm the only one who gets a say in the matter. I don't know any of you and I haven't asked you for anything, which is fine since you don't want to give it anyway."

I could feel the tears welling up in my eyes and I cursed these fucking pregnancy hormones for making me so irrational. "I don't need your help." The bedroom was fourteen short steps away and I made my escape.

Fucking men. They were a useless lot in my experience and I should have known better than to expect more from this group. They were cut from the same cloth as Genesis, just a little less psycho. I fell to the bed as the twist of irony stabbed my gut. Tears streaked down my cheeks at the unfairness of it all, left for me to deal with my younger, dumber self. How sad was it that I was wishing for more time to wallow in self-pity?

I sat up and tried to clear my mind so I could think through my options. It would be easier to go without Lasso, but my odds were better with him by my side. Was it fair to use him like that? Probably not, but I'd given him every chance to back out so now we were stuck together.

The door opened and closed and I felt the bed sink under Lasso's weight. "I'm sorry, Rocky. They don't mean to hurt your feelings."

"I get it, I really do. But if you say they're just looking out for me one more fucking time I'll rip this baby out of me and beat you with it!"

He froze and when I peeked up at him a slow smile spread across my face.

"I can't believe you threatened that! Crazy woman."

That pulled a laugh out of me. "I meant what I said. I'm not taking any damn test and I don't blame them for not helping. And I won't blame you if you've changed your mind."

"Don't fucking say that, not ever." There was a steel in his voice I'd never heard before. "I'm in. All in. Tomorrow we'll go get married. Jag's working out the details for our honeymoon."

"We don't need a honeymoon."

I knew this wasn't a real marriage and I hoped he wouldn't pretend otherwise under some false sense of nobility.

"Maybe, maybe not." He shrugged like it was no big deal, but I could see the delight and mischief swimming in those sky-blue eyes. "But we do need to lie low for a little while, right?"

"Sure."

"Okay. So Jag is working on someplace secure, and we'll call it a honeymoon. And I need you to listen to me Rocky. You need to trust that I wasn't born yesterday, and I know what the fuck I'm talking about."

I laughed because he wouldn't be the first man in my life to make that claim. "Fine, but that goes both ways. I'm not the little pregnant lady. I am a capable, independent being and your partner. Partner, got it?"

"You are little and you are a lady, but yeah I got it. Now come over here and seal this little deal of ours with a kiss."

I happily rolled on top of him and pressed my mouth to his, licking his lips, his tongue before taking over his whole mouth. I couldn't get enough of him. Maybe it was the hormones or maybe it was the man, but whenever he was close it was never close enough. I kissed him until I was breathless and my brow was damp with sweat as I ground against him, feeling him harden between my legs.

"Lasso. The things I dream of doing to that mouth."

"I'm saving myself for marriage sweetheart so keep those dreams on ice until tomorrow, all right?"

I pouted and he laughed, smacking my ass.

"But after we say 'I do' all bets are off."

I found that both intriguing and wildly satisfying.

***

"I now pronounce you man and wife, now go on and keep that hunk-a burnin' love alive and kiss your bride."

Yep, I totally went for the Elvis wedding because, why the hell not? I might never get married again but I'll always have a photo of me in a wedding dress with Elvis at my side.

"My favorite part." Lasso smiled wide as he pulled me in and kissed me like we hadn't woken up in each other's arms two and a half hours ago, lips and bodies locked tight. It was one hell of a kiss.

"Like my mama used to say, start as you intend to go on." Just to prove his point he kissed me again. "Mrs. Cooper."

"Mrs. Izzo-Cooper," I corrected. We were married but it wasn't for love so I wouldn't lose my identity, not even temporarily. "If that kiss is a preview of this marriage, I approve."

"Good because next is more foreplay."

His smile was so playful it almost felt real, like we were just two impulsive people who decided to get up early as fuck and get married.

"Making out in the back of a limo?"

"No, food. Watching you eat always gets me hard." He leaned into the crook of my neck, his voice vibrating as his tongue snaked out to taste me.

"There's no limo though, our honeymoon is a bit more rustic than that."

"Rustic?"

Lasso heard the squeak in my voice and laughed, forcing me to bug him all through our celebratory wedding breakfast and even as we got on the road. He'd almost distracted me completely, until we crossed into Idaho. And kept driving. "By the way, where did you get this car? Is it stolen?"

"It's not stolen, Ro."

"Don't laugh at me."

"I'm not," he insisted, pretending to lock up his words and throw away the key. "You really think I'm dumb enough to go into hiding with a car people will actively be looking for? I'm hurt."

"No, of course not. Sorry. But you won't tell me anything." It was childish to keep asking when I knew my safety was his only goal. "Tell me more about your family, Lasso. I know you're from Rose Petal, Texas. I know all about running off to join the military to spite them. But you're not telling me everything."

Lasso let out a sigh like somebody'd just put the screws to him and he had to cave. "So, okay. What you need to understand is, my family is pretty big shit due to our big ol' ranch and contribution to the steak and potatoes atmosphere around town. We own about half the town which makes my family think they can tell us all how to live."

"Judgmental?"

He shrugged. "They just think they know best about everything. Including my life. That's why I left."

"And went to the military. Got that." There were more layers to Lasso than I thought and that didn't bode well for me. Pregnant, hormonal and on the run with a kind and handsome man who knew how to give me the best orgasms I ever had. What could possibly go wrong except everything?

"I joined because I always wanted to, and I planned to ever since Billy Macready's father came to speak to our class in the fourth grade. Mama thought I'd grow out of it and Daddy just assumed that I wouldn't dare defy him. They were both wrong."

## Wonderfully Wrecked

I looked at him, at the tightly coiled tension beneath his laidback outer shell. He didn't like talking about his family, but he was doing it, for me. "How'd you get the nickname Lasso?"

"You don't want to know," he grumbled.

I pushed but he kept quiet, even when I put my hand high on his thigh, letting my pinky graze his sac. "If it's not about cowboy stuff it must be because you're such a big ol' whore, right?"

"Whore?" He choked on the word but he couldn't hide the amused smile on his face. "Did you just call me a big ol' whore?"

"I did. So, which is it?"

"Neither, but now my feelings are hurt and I'm not inclined to tell you the real story."

He was so full of shit and I proved it my nibbling on his ear as he turned down a mostly dirt road covered with thick, green trees.

"I call bullshit," I said before he made another turn and a big ass cabin came into view but only once we were deep in the thick of the trees.

I swallowed at the big pine structure and fell against my seat. It was two stories with dark windows all around and a big wraparound porch. It looked like how rich people roughed it. "Is this yours?"

"It belongs to the club." He said it so simply, like motorcycle clubs just owned mansions in the woods.

"Business must be good." Because I never remember Dad having that kind of money after a score.

"You know the biggest outlaws do business legally, don't you?"

"I do." It made me happy to hear that the Reckless Bastards had legitimate businesses, but I wondered about something else. "Does your family know yet they're about to gain another member?"

"No, but it's not because of you. It's because of them. I'll tell them, I promise. Eventually. Does your dad know?"

"Nope. I don't even know where he is and it's probably safe that he doesn't know."

We were a pair. How could we be parents with such terrible role models? We were both good people, so I had hope for this baby growing in my belly. If he or she made it to term, it had a pretty good shot at becoming a decent human being. I hoped. "So, this is our honeymoon suite? I didn't know you cared so much, husband."

He smirked and dropped a hand on my thigh, stroking slowly, making me moan. "You're a smartass."

"That's my most charming personality trait," I insisted. "Regretting you didn't get a quieter model?"

He laughed and jumped from the car, jogging around the front and pulling me out. "Nah, I like you best when you're loud." He kissed me again like I was someone else. Someone special and precious to him. Like I mattered.

It really was too bad I couldn't keep Lasso.

He was exactly my kind of perfect.

## Chapter 16

*Lasso*

"This isn't exactly rustic," Rocky grumbled at the same time I argued, "You said you couldn't cook."

My tone wasn't accusatory as we dug into the smoky, spicy chili she'd whipped up when we arrived a couple of hours ago. Just surprised. "And I said it was *more* rustic than a tropical honeymoon vacation."

She looked around the kitchen, at the exposed beams across the ceiling and the pine and chrome everywhere. Her gaze landed on the Sub-zero fridge, then the six-top stove with double ovens, and finally a large butcher top table with high backed wooden chairs.

"It's the fanciest thing I've ever seen called rustic." She paused and looked around again. "But I like it. It's homey despite being big as hell."

"You got something against big things?" She rolled her eyes as I knew she would.

"No, but I thought we'd be hiding out in some tiny one room cabin and calling it a honeymoon to soothe your ego. Not this," she said as she waved her hands round the room. She realized her tone might be a tough offensive and sighed before turning back to me. "Sorry. This is great, I'm just … hell I don't know, but thank you Lasso."

"No problem. Wife." It was still weird saying that, but it got easier and I loved getting a rise out of Rocky. Even a little one. "This chili is damn good for someone who can't cook."

"Thanks. And I never said I couldn't cook. I said don't expect me to cook." Her shoulders had relaxed a little bit with each passing hour. But so far, I couldn't do a damn thing to erase the worry from her eyes. "Do you eat at the clubhouse and if so, do you have a cook there?"

I laughed because it was just such a Rocky question. Most women wanted to know about illegal activities and fights and shit but she wanted to know about housekeeping.

"I usually eat at home and, no, there's no cook there. If we're on lockdown or some shit, the women and the Bitches will cook but otherwise we feed ourselves."

"Bummer. Seems like a good way to make use of a vet who's not cut out for the other stuff."

"What other stuff?" I could tell something about the Reckless Bastards bothered her, but I didn't know if it was just because they were unwilling to help or something more.

"You know what I mean, stuff like shooting a gun or whooping some ass. Or what about a guy who stutters? Can't have him working at the gun range or the dispensary but maybe he's a crack shot. Or the guy who's good with numbers but can't ride a bike to save his life."

Yeah, she caught me, but Rocky didn't smirk or brag about it. And she made her point. "You have to ride. That's why it's called a motorcycle club."

"What's organized socialization without arbitrary rules?" She pushed her bowl away and rubbed her belly. "And it's time for me to lie down before I doze off sitting here."

I watched her go, enjoying the sway of her hips and feeling a little disappointed I wouldn't be getting any wedding night sex. The pregnancy was wearing on her in a thousand little ways, but she hadn't complained about it yet. After rinsing the dishes, I joined Rocky on the sofa, lifting her head and putting it on my lap.

"If you're trying to get head, I'm game but you gotta do all the work."

A laugh bubbled up out of me at her words. "You're kind of crazy, aren't you?"

"Doesn't matter now, you married me." She moaned as my fingers sifted through her hair, snuggling deeper into my lap. She had to notice my cock hardening beneath her head but the champ that she was, Rocky ignored it. "Did you have a horse as a kid?"

"I did. Windsor, an appaloosa, you know with a spotted coat? Mom thought it looked regal so she named him Windsor." Her laugh was pure and amused. "He was wild and energetic, perfect for a little boy. We'd rip around the property together as fast as we could, trying to outrun the wind."

"Sounds nice. Why did you leave?"

"Too many expectations I had no plans on living up to. It won't ever stop so I removed myself from the equation."

"Do you ever regret it?"

I thought about her question as I often did over the years. "No. I mean I wish they could've been happy with who I wanted to be or maybe that I could've been happy being who they wanted for a son, but I don't regret leaving."

Her eyes wandered over the high ceiling as if she were looking for some truth up there before she spoke. "Me either. I miss my dad sometimes, but I've spent most of my life missing him, so I'm used to it." Her sigh was heavy but she didn't move, just lay there while my hands got lost in her thick red hair. "Do you wish I hadn't tracked you down?"

I sighed at her question and kept running my fingers through her hair, massaging her scalp with my fingertips.

*Do I wish she hadn't tracked me down?*

"No Rocky, I don't. I'm glad you thought I was the kind of guy you could come to when trouble found you. I'm sorry you're in the middle of this shit show but I don't regret you showing up on my doorstep, not one damn bit." I felt like a fool for saying all that to her but when I risked a glance at Rocky her eyes were closed and her breathing had evened out.

She was asleep.

# Wonderfully Wrecked

It was for the best anyway. I hoped she hadn't heard that verbal diarrhea because she didn't need to hear it. She was here under my protection, she and our baby, and that's what mattered most. It wasn't her feelings or mine that mattered, just keeping her safe. My wife and kid. What a fucking trip to think of those two words in reference to me. The fucked up part was this was exactly what my folks wanted for me, a wife and a kid, though they'd probably shit their pants that I'd married a sexy bohemian who made a living selling craft items.

A laugh bubbled up out of me at the irony of them getting what they wanted in the most wrong way possible. There was a kind of twisted beauty to it that made me want to get up right now and tell them. But more than that, I was content where I was. Oddly so. Sitting on the ugly ass sofa Jag had insisted we put in here for 'local flavor' with my arm on the wooden rest and the soft weight of Rocky's head in my lap, it all felt right.

More fucking right than anything had in a long time.

What that said about me and the predicament I was in, I didn't even want to think about. Instead, I stood and picked up Rocky, enjoying those soft feminine curves as I tucked us both into bed, watching the stars pop in the sky through the huge bedroom window while she slept curled into my side.

***

I woke up the next morning to the smell of peppers and maple. "Ah, shit!" And the sound of Rocky swearing enough to make a sailor blush. With a laugh I kicked off the blankets and swung my legs around to the floor, smiling at her colorful language before going to the bathroom.

When I came out and joined Rocky in the kitchen, my shorts grew tight at the sight of her in nothing but a thin cotton t-shirt. "Breakfast and a show. I approve."

Startled, she turned with a glare that quickly morphed into a smile. "Hey, you look normal."

"Uh, thanks Rocky. You look good enough to eat." She blushed prettily, and I went to the counter where coffee sat black and steaming. "Can pregnant chicks drink coffee?"

"No, but that doesn't mean you can't. Smoking is where I have to draw the line." She looked wary and apologetic, but I could see how important it was to her.

"Other than a little grass, I don't smoke and I'm happy to do it outside."

Rocky's smile was soft and feminine. It took everything in me to let her bring the food to the table instead of clearing the whole thing to make room for her. "Good. With the fucked up environment we have around us now, I want to keep things as clean as possible."

She was so serious and fierce in protecting our child that I wrapped my arms around her.

"That kid is going to be the luckiest fucker alive to have you for a mama, Rocky." She let out a tinkling laugh with her arms snaked around my waist, careful to keep the hot spatula away from my back.

"That's *our* kid, the lucky fucker," she murmured into my neck.

"You know what I mean, it smells incredible in here." Like food and family. "Reminds me of Lulu; she was our cook my whole life. Made the best damn bacon I ever had."

"So, you miss Lulu?" She smiled again and pulled back to take her seat at the table.

"I guess I do. I hadn't really thought about it—or her—in years." I worked pretty damn hard not to remember much about Rose Petal. "The town was a great place to grow up, be stupid and not fuck up your whole life. But otherwise I'm happy I live in Mayhem."

"An appropriate name for your lot." This time she said it with amusement rather than her usual wariness.

"We get up to trouble when we have to, otherwise we're mostly just brothers."

"No offense Lasso but I've seen brothers throw in because someone said the wrong thing to a guy's woman and your *brothers* won't step up for you. With family like that, makes me glad I'm on my own."

She was right in a way and I understood her perspective. "Except you're not on your own, are you? There's me and that baby in your belly. I'm sorry if that's not enough, but it's all we have." I felt annoyed that she didn't think I was enough, angry too. And it felt so fucking familiar I couldn't finish my breakfast.

"It's not that you're not enough, Lasso. This is my problem and without your club's help the chances that you'll end up hurt because of me only increases and I can't deal with that. Not right now." She shoved her own plate away angrily and stood. "I have to ... go," she said and distractedly left the kitchen.

I decided to give Rocky some time on her own to get a handle on her emotions. Twenty minutes later I had the kitchen clean and I was just about ready to go after Rocky when my phone rang.

I knew who it would be, so I didn't bother looking at the screen. "What's up, Cross?"

"How are you guys doing?"

"Fine. You got any news?" I knew that was the only reason he'd call while we were up here.

"Yeah," he sighed. "Big Boy took a while to crack but once that fucker opened up, he was a flood of info."

"Good. Anything we can actually use?"

Cross sighed heavily but I ignored it, waiting impatiently while I got busy in the kitchen, getting shit ready for a picnic.

"Just one thing. Says Genesis is sending guys in waves, every couple days until the fourteen days are up. If she doesn't show up in time for the heist, bad shit."

I heard what he was and wasn't saying. "Right. Has anyone showed up yet?"

He waited a beat before answering. "Not that we can tell but everyone is on high alert."

"She's not going, Cross but we'll head back tomorrow night." Rocky needed more time away from the stress of the city so tomorrow night would give her more time and allow us the cover of night to roll into town.

Another fucking pause. I rolled my eyes and continued making sandwiches with the phone tucked under my ear. I packed a cooler with the sandwiches, some water and fruit while I waited for Cross to figure out some diplomatic way to say whatever was working its way through his brain.

Finally he came back to me with, "Are you sure she can't do this one job?"

He was like a fucking broken record. I took a deep breath and held it for a second, then let it out, filled with all the things I wouldn't say to him because there would be no going back. I tried my best to keep my voice even. "No, Cross, she can't and I can't even believe you'd fucking ask me that. She would hate that

I'm telling you this and I'm only doing this so you can fucking see why."

I told him about the asshole giving her coke for her friends and then charging her for it so he could get her to work it off.

"What do you think she would've been doing if she hadn't happened to have this unique skill? Jesus, would you have asked Lauren to do that?"

He growled into the phone and I could just imagine the anger coursing through him. "Never. But Lauren never would have dated that asshole."

I wanted to throw the phone at the wall. Or worse. But I just said, "You mean she never would have gotten with the head of a criminal organization?" It was an asshole move to get sarcastic about it, but he was being a dick. "Right. Of course she wouldn't."

"Fuck you, Lasso."

"No, fuck you, Cross! She's carrying my kid and you just want me to hand her over to a psychopath? Yeah, fuck you too."

## Wonderfully Wrecked

I ended the call and squeezed the phone so tight it came close to cracking.

"That sounded like it went well."

I turned to glare at Rocky, but she'd changed into a flimsy little dress that made her tits look like a dream. "We're going fishing."

She frowned and then smiled. "Are you serious?" When I nodded she squealed, clapped and turned, running back up the stairs. I could hear the patter of her feet and I smiled. It was nice to see her smiling again. For a minute she looked like the girl I met on the beach in San Diego.

Within minutes she was back, chirping, "Okay I'm ready."

She stood there wearing a giddy grin and the same dress but a floppy hat now covered her head and she held a straw bag under her arm.

"Come on, I've got lunch."

"Good because someone ruined my breakfast."

Her lips twitched when I looked over my shoulder at her while I locked the door. "Thank you," she moaned when I reached into the cooler on the way to the lake and handed her a sausage and egg sandwich. She tore into it and moaned even louder with the first bite.

"I wasn't trying to ruin your breakfast Rocky, but it's shitty for you to keep saying you're alone when you've got me."

She stopped in the dirt path and turned to me. "I know you feel responsible for me because of the baby, Lasso, but I can't help but feel guilty about dragging you into my shit show. It's not about diminishing your importance here." She sighed, frustrated and marched toward the dock with her shoulders hanging low.

The bass boat was where it always was and in a few minutes, I had helped her into a seat. I took the seat opposite her and fired up the motor and before we knew it we were in the middle of the small lake.

"Have you ever fished?" I asked?

# Wonderfully Wrecked

"A few times with my dad but I was about eight or nine." She looked around at the scenery with the willows and thick green grass along the overgrown plots of land before she turned back to me. She grabbed the hem of her dress and pulled it over her head to reveal a pink bikini with white daisies. I tried to keep my gaze on the water, but we were alone and Rocky was lathering her arms, legs, chest and back with sunscreen.

"Take off your shirt," she ordered.

I looked over at her, a mix of adorable and sexy in her barely there bikini, pregnant belly and windblown hair.

"Sure thing, sweetheart, but maybe wait until we anchor down someplace," I bit back a grin at the sexy scowl that shot straight to my cock and then my shirt was crawling up my body. "I like it when you're feisty."

"You have mental issues. We'll have to enroll the baby in therapy right away."

Her words put an image in my mind of a little kid, old enough to walk but still kind of wobbly and like that the pregnancy became real to me. That baby in her belly became a person.

We puttered along lazily in the hot sun for a few minutes, sitting next to each other but lost in our own thoughts. And then . . .

"Ho-ly shit!" I screamed.

Something cold and slick hit my back and Rocky laughed.

"Sun protection, cowboy," she said, but her hands lingered all over my back and around my waist, sliding slow and sexy along my abs. "And maybe a little bit of copping a feel."

"A little?"

"Hey, I'm just don't want you to get skin cancer."

We both laughed. "You were so close to sounding sincere too."

"I know, dammit. Turn around."

## Wonderfully Wrecked

I made her wait until we reached one of my favorite fishing spots before I exposed my body to her.

"There, now you can put your hands all over me." She took her sweet time and I swear I nearly came in my shorts and would have if she'd brushed my nipple one more time. "All right, dirty girl. Now we fish."

We worked in silence for a long time, first setting up our rods over the side and then waiting. Always waiting. The patience I learned fishing as a boy helped me as a soldier where there was even more fuckin' waiting. Though the silence was comfortable, even companionable, I wanted to talk. To hear her sweet voice and that sexy laugh.

"I got one!" she yelped.

I leaned forward, ready to help her from her perch opposite me when she held up her prize: a colorful bass.

"Great catch!" I said, proud as I could be.

Her skin was flushed pink with excitement and her smile spread wide across her gorgeous face.

"Thanks! That was as fun as I remember." She winced and grabbed her belly and I was at her side in an instant. "I'm fine. I'm fine. I think I woke up the baby that's all. But I'll rest a bit, give you time to catch up."

"There's food in the cooler, fruit and water too."

"Aww look at you being a mother hen," she joked and poked me in the side until I laughed. "Thank you, Lasso. Seriously."

"Believe me, it is a pleasure to watch you eat." She rolled her eyes and shifted her gaze toward the water, smiling contentedly at the slight wake the boat made as we floated over the surface and the birds flying along the tide. Eventually I added two more bass to the bounty while Rocky chatted about nothing and fed me.

"I don't want to ruin this wonderful day but, we need to talk."

"Words no man, or husband, ever wants to hear."

She smacked my arm. "Quiet, buster. Seriously though, it sounds like your boss isn't in the mood to help, which means we need to be creative. When I was still in San Diego and they were trying to do things the nice way, Big Boy told me that a couple of their stash houses were hit. That's where Genesis keeps most of his money."

"I thought you weren't all that involved in his business?" I hadn't meant to sound so accusatory, but it came out that way.

"I wasn't but I would be in the car when he made a stop to all these random houses in sketchy neighborhoods. I'm not stupid, Lasso." She rolled her eyes and wrapped her arms around her body protectively.

"Look, if you don't trust me just say so now and you can drop me off at the nearest city and I'll be fine. On my own."

"It was just a fucking question. And stop. We're in this together."

She closed her eyes and took several deep breaths but when Rocky opened her eyes they weren't on me, they were on the water.

"We need to make him crazy so he makes a mistake, that's where we find our advantage. Hit more of his stash houses until he's desperate for cash, for firepower. For control."

"You propose we carpool to LA to steal from your ex? That's your plan?"

"No, my plan is for us to sell this information to people who wouldn't mind seeing Genesis taken down. They'll happily knock over a stash house and they'll get plenty of joy from it if it's a rival and they get to keep the stash."

It wasn't a bad plan, actually. "He won't realize it's us, though."

"So? Are you so macho that he needs to? The point isn't that he knows it's us, the point is to fuck him. Hit him where it hurts, steadily and consistently until he's cut off at the knees." She still wouldn't look at me and even though I deserved it, I hated it.

"Well?" She asked me, impatiently.

"How pissed are you right now? You know what, it doesn't matter." I grabbed her by the waist and pulled her onto my lap, kissing her before she had a chance to react. She tasted like grapes and pineapple and I couldn't get enough of those plump lips and that succulent tongue. The way she squirmed and tried to get closer, spearing her hands through my hair, had my cock standing up tall and ready to invade.

Rocky pulled back first wearing a mile wide grin. "Just because you kiss like that doesn't mean you're not still an asshole."

"I know. But I was hoping the kiss would remind you of all my good qualities."

She sighed and moved away. "I know you're a good man."

"But?" Because I could hear the 'but' coming a mile away.

"But none of this is real and I don't want to fight with you like a couple, because we're not a real couple. You married me for the baby just like you're keeping me safe for the baby. I appreciate it, but I can't pretend. We can have sex and talk and all that, but let's not do the rest of that, okay?"

Well, shit. That didn't end the way I thought it would.

Fuck.

## Chapter 17

*Rocky*

Fishing had been both a pleasure and a pain in my ass because it highlighted what I already knew. Lasso didn't trust me. Still. Not that he should, but he shouldn't mistrust me so much. But there was nothing I could do about it, so as soon as we made it back to the cabin I ran a bath to help me relax.

I probably shouldn't have unloaded on Lasso the way I did. He didn't deserve it when he was only being honest. I overreacted because this little peanut inside of me wreaked havoc on my hormones. There was no way in hell I would apologize, though. I was the one coming up with plans while he begged his so called "brothers and friends" for help they weren't inclined to give.

*Ugh, whatever!* This wasn't what I came into the bathroom to think about, so I stepped into the hot water and leaned back with my eyes closed, letting the water carry away my stress and worries. At least temporarily.

I had to focus on one problem at a time. And despite my good intentions, a list began to form in my head of people who'd love to have a hand in taking down Genesis. I needed to reach out to them as soon as I could. Then I had to figure out my next move.

A knock sounded and then Lasso popped his head into the room. "Hey. Need a hand?"

The man didn't give up. Not yet, anyway but I knew there would come a time. Probably sooner rather than later. "I'm good Lasso, thanks."

"Come on Rocky, I'm trying to apologize. I was being an asshole earlier." He shoved both hands through his hair and blew out a breath. "This is hard for me too."

I knew that. His friends were his family and they all doubted me, it was only natural those doubts would surface in him. "I know and that's why I think we should keep things separate, the sex and the rest of it."

## Wonderfully Wrecked

"We're married Rocky, there is no rest of it, just us and our lives."

I shook my head, unable to accept that answer. "We're married *for the baby*, Lasso. Not because you love me and want to spend the rest of your life with me, but because someone will likely kill me before this is all over. This doesn't make you a bad guy. It just is what it is."

He was about to argue, I could see it in those big blue eyes but then all the tension left his body. And a sultry smile crossed his face. "Fine. Then I'm apologizing for being a prick earlier and I want to make it up to you. By helping with your bath."

"Not necessary."

"Maybe," he said and pushed off the wall to come closer and sit beside the tub, draping one arm over the side so his fingertips brushed the sudsy water. "Or maybe it's very necessary." His hand scraped along the water and then over my knee, up my thigh coming so fucking close to my pussy only to cross over and drag down the opposite leg. "So I'm going to wash you, Rocky, all of you. And then I'm going to do things."

"Things?" I arched my brow, intrigued

"Things Rocky. Things with my mouth."

I *loved* those things. I should have just opened my mouth and told him no, smacked his hand away and kicked him out. But I couldn't. I didn't because I was putty in his very capable hands. "How could I resist that?"

"I'm glad you can't." He wore a confident smile as he lathered his hands up with my body wash. "I'll never think of anything but you anytime I smell this combination of flowers and sex."

"Sex? It's sandalwood and wild flowers."

"Whatever it is, I love it." He washed my legs, my arms and my back in slow, drugging circles. He took his sweet time when it came to washing my tits, stroking and cupping them until I moaned, tweaking my nipples until I was gasping in pleasure.

"Not as much as those sounds though." His fingers slid between my legs and rubbed back and forth.

"Oh, fuck!" Two fingers slid deep, curving to hit me in the spot that made my whole body light up. My chest heaved, and my breaths came out in sharp pants as he thrust deep and rubbed my clit until my body jerked with an orgasm. "Lasso!"

"Yes, wife?"

I laughed and leaned my head back, enjoying the way his fingertips grazed along my sensitized skin. "That feels good."

And just when I thought things couldn't get better, he tilted my head back and washed my hair. He *washed my hair*! My mom was the last person to wash my hair who wasn't me and that was the night before she split for good. It was nice even if it conjured up a few memories I thought I'd cleared away years ago.

He soaped it up into a good lather, his fingertips working my scalp until I let out a loud, erotic moan. "God that feels so good."

He chuckled and rinsed my hair, lifting me out of the tub and I felt like I was floating on a cloud. "You'll be saying that a lot tonight."

"Promises, promises."

"Guaranteed, honey. Satisfaction guaranteed."

Lasso dried me off and I never felt so pampered in all my life. "Now let's talk about these mouth things."

"Let's not," he said and took one step back. Then another, and another as he slowly undressed, seducing me with his big blue eyes. He dropped one knee on the bed and then the other, lying right down the middle. "Let's just do it. Come here Rocky, come show me what you want me to do to you with my mouth."

Who in the hell was I to pass up an offer like that? I'd been dreaming of riding his face like I had that first night in San Diego ever since I crossed the Nevada border. Sooner, if I'm being totally honest. And when I climbed on the bed and saw that sexy, knowing smirk and the way he licked his lips, I straddled his chest. "Anything?"

"I'm adventurous. Just try not to suffocate me."

I was too hot and wet and horny to wonder if it was because I was fat. "Fine, no air restricting sex gymnastics. Got it. Anything else?"

He nodded. "Make it dirty?"

"I can do that." And I did, holding on to the headboard with a firm grip, I rode and ground against his tongue that moved like it was battery operated. This position was hotter than I remembered and the sounds he made, so wet and so … slurpy. So damn hot I thought I might come before this party even got started properly. It felt so good. Too good.

"Lasso," I moaned and sat back so I could look at him. I looked down at those blue eyes and rode his mouth and tongue and chin and nose like it was my only job in this word, using Lasso's face to get off.

And I did get off.

Hard.

And when I felt one long finger, wet with my juices slip between my ass cheeks, I pushed back into it, grinding in both directions until my body was just one big vessel of sensations and feelings. The vibrating started at my toes and moved its way up, slow and sizzling. My hips rocked faster, harder as he thrust in and out with a slow, practiced ease that left me feeling full and turned on to the point of discomfort.

"Oh fuck! Lasso!"

He sucked my clit and my hips bucked up into him. The moan he let out rocked through me and yanked the orgasm from my body on a loud, pulsating roar.

And then I rolled off him and collapsed. "Damn that mouth!"

"Thanks, sugar, but I gotta say, the pleasure was all mine."

## Wonderfully Wrecked

I doubted that because I was riding on a wave of pleasure and satisfaction and boneless bliss that I had never felt before. Ever. "Not possible, baby daddy."

He laughed. "That's husband baby daddy to you."

There was that word again. *Husband.* I had just used my husband like a scratching post and I had no regrets. "Fine. But now it's your turn. Husband."

He smacked my ass and growled. "I love it when you talk dirty to me."

It took a while, but I managed. I'd finally found something dirty enough to make my hardened, biker baby daddy blush.

~~~

"Do you have some place set for us to stay when we get back? Because your house is not an option at the moment."

Lasso hadn't told me everything about his conversation with Cross but since he didn't argue, it was safe to assume they'd been there. Again.

Lasso looked out at the lake beyond, his tall form casting long shadows across the placid body of water and splashing it in the color of the setting sun. His body appeared relaxed, but I could see the tension gathered at the corners of his mouth and eyes, the white-knuckle grip he had on his water bottle.

"The club is our best option because we can control all entry points and there are rooms and three little apartments above the hangar."

I didn't relish the idea of staying with a bunch of people who would just sit around and watch once the shit hit the fan but Lasso was right, it was the best option.

"You wouldn't happen to have blueprints, would you?" It was a completely ridiculous question considering we were sitting out on the back deck, eating bass with fries and vegetables, not to mention

## Wonderfully Wrecked

the fact that we'd left Mayhem in a hurry with less than the essentials.

"You know, Rocky, I left them in my other jeans."

"Smart ass," I grumbled and stole a piece of broccoli from his plate.

"Are you still hungry?" He was up on his feet before I could answer, scooping more fish and vegetables onto my plate. "Eat up."

"Bossy too," I said but I gobbled up the flaky fish and the vegetables because with every day that passed my hunger only grew.

"I know, right? Too bad you're stuck with me." He grinned and shoved a fry in my mouth when I opened it to curse at him. "No Rocky, I don't have any blueprints or floor plans, but we'll be there in a few hours and I promise to give you a full tour, okay?"

It wasn't okay because it meant I'd be planning in a hurry and I didn't like that, but he didn't have what I needed so I nodded. "Fine." My plate was clean and there was just a sliver of sun left before we were covered in darkness. "Thank you for this, Lasso. For these few days of no stress, good food and really good sex. It was a nice little bubble."

"It was and if you give me some bullshit 'save yourself' speech, you and me are gonna have problems. Got it?"

"Why haven't you considered it, Lasso? Really?" He was stubborn as hell and while I appreciated it, it baffled me.

"Because you came to me for help, Rocky. You showed up on my doorstep in need of help and I don't care about anything else but being worthy of the trust you put in me. Okay?"

His words shocked the hell out of me. All this time I thought he was some sort of control freak, eager to keep me under his thumb. I felt like an asshole because he was just an honorable guy.

Who happened to be in a biker gang. I mean motorcycle club.

"Yeah, okay Lasso. So, I'll do the kitchen and you do the heavy lifting?" We needed to pack and get on the road and I would use cleaning to steel my nerves and clear my head for whatever came next.

"Maybe you ought to stay off your feet. I don't want you getting tired and worn out when we already have so much to worry about."

I rolled my eyes and resisted the urge to smile at his bossy worrying. "I'm perfectly capable of handling washing a few dishes and scrubbing a few counters, Lasso. If you get all delicate on me now, we're in trouble."

He stood in front of me, hands gripping the arms of my chair so I was trapped between him and my seat. It wasn't a bad place to be.

"It's not delicate to be concerned, Rocky. And since I know you won't tell me how you're feeling, I'm going to ask."

Before I could respond, his lips brushed against mine, gently at first and then more insistent. He swallowed my moan and pulled back.

"And I'm going to keep asking until I'm sure you're okay. Deal with it."

His lips pressed against mine again, harder this time until I opened up and he slipped his sweet tongue in, tasting of barbecue sauce and root beer.

It was the kind of kiss that would have led to a lot of dirty things if we had the time. Which we didn't. Dammit.

"Go. We have to deal with this."

Lasso pressed his forehead to mine and groaned. "I know. I wish I could keep you up here until this was over."

"And I wish I'd never brought this to your door." If he ended up hurt because of me, how could I forgive myself? How would our child forgive me?

## Wonderfully Wrecked

"I wish you never knew guys like Genesis existed." It was sincere and heartfelt, proving once again that Lasso really was one of the good ones.

"I'm glad you showed me there are a few good ones still out there."

His grin turned playful. "And lucky you, all this is yours."

For now. "Make it snappy and maybe I'll give you road head."

"Damn wife, you should have led with that," he smirked, whistling cheerfully as he carried the dishes into the kitchen. I sat there for a minute, just watching him move. Lasso was a real man, not just big and strong but capable and kind. He would make a good husband and dad. For some other woman.

I would do everything I could to get us out of this.

That meant I needed to get off my pregnant ass and get my shit together. I had things to order, phone calls to make and a very nice gourmet kitchen to clean.

Seventy minutes later we were on the road, driving through rural Idaho, which was basically *all* of Idaho, literally under the cover of darkness.

"What are you doing over there?" he asked after we had a bunch of miles behind us.

"I'm sketching out a map of LA by territory. It would be reckless to have gangs going into other gang territory to raid a stash house when they likely have one in their own territory."

He snickered. "Looking out for the gangbangers of greater Los Angeles?"

"No, the innocent people those assholes are likely to shoot because they don't practice."

Things couldn't have changed that much but doing this on the fly meant they were all best guesses.

"Now, keep quiet while I make some calls."

It took longer than I thought, which was a miscalculation on my part. Convincing my contacts I wasn't running a scam had taken some time. But they were all intrigued and I could hear the glee they couldn't hide, and that's how I knew this plan would work.

"That was some skilled negotiations."

Lasso sounded impressed and I was pretty sure there was pride shining in his eyes when he smiled over at me.

"Do you think they bought it?"

"Not fully, but they'll send some guys low on the totem pole to scope it out and then they'll strike. If what your friend Cross says is true, that he's sending guys in waves, the houses will be unprotected or at least with a smaller crew."

I hated that I still knew this shit but being zoned out on pills and pot hadn't diminished my ability to absorb info.

"So now we wait?"

"Now we drive to your hangar, sleep, eat and prepare."

It had to stop, and I had to figure out a way to make it happen before anyone else got hurt.

# Chapter 18

*Lasso*

It took us two days to make the drive because I wanted to stick to the road at night and because I couldn't let Rocky sleep in the car, not after all the work she'd done to set things in motion. It was unbelievable really, the way her mind worked. She could've been an evil genius in her own right if she had the temperament for the outlaw life.

Then again, she still needed to get used to my life with the Reckless Bastards. She hadn't said as much but I could tell Rocky's views hadn't changed much and the guys hadn't done shit to help change her mind. I just had to hope that I would be enough to change it.

"Sounds like there's a party going on." Rocky's hand tightened in mine as we arrived at the club and her steps grew slower, more cautious.

I clocked the guys standing out front and the closed gates meant that some shit had gone down. "Hey guys, what's going on?"

Stitch stopped twiddling with his moustache and grinned.

"Hey Lasso man, glad to see you're in one piece. We're on lockdown. Some fucktards broke into your house and then showed up at Mandy's store, breaking shit and threatening her. Worst of fucking all, they tried to knock off the Mayhem & Medicine Dispensary. I fuckin' love that place, man."

I held back a smirk. Stitch was equal parts teenage boy, efficient killer and weapons expert. "Did they get anything?"

"Nothing besides a fuckin' beat down. Cross and the guys are inside." He stepped aside, and I ushered Rocky in ahead of me though she stuck close to my side, leaving barely any room between us. Not that I was complaining.

"Thanks, Stitch."

## Wonderfully Wrecked

I didn't bother with an introduction because I was sure he knew who Rocky was. I didn't know his opinion on the situation and I didn't give a damn. Inside really was like a party, but lockdowns always were. There were several tables piled high with food, tubs of beer buried in ice, one of the newest brothers worked the bar and the Reckless Bitches made sure the guys were distracted. In the corner were Teddy, Mandy and Jana with their babies.

"Lockdown?"

"All the family comes here so we can deploy resources to protect our interests."

Rocky looked around, eyes as wide as saucers before turning them back up to me. "Can I have a gun?"

I smiled. "Do you know how to use a gun?"

She rolled her eyes at me and for a moment I felt like we were a real couple. "Like you don't remember Max gave me lessons?"

"Of course I do. But can you shoot in your condition?"

Bonehead move. I could practically see the steam coming out of her ears. "Okay, fine. If you're sure. I'll get you a gun."

"Granted my accuracy isn't the greatest," she added "but I can wound with the best of 'em."

With all hell breaking loose around us, Rocky could still make me laugh. "You're so damn cute when you get all southern gunslinger on me," I said, wanting to take her somewhere private right then and really show my appreciation. But I just whispered in her ear and said, "Okay, yes, I'll get you a gun."

"Thanks, and don't get me some bullshit piece like a .22, I'm warning you." She groaned and stepped back. Seconds later I could see why.

"You're back," Cross said, Savior at his side.

"I am. No trouble to report on our end. How's my place looking?"

"Like shit," Savior said. "They clearly didn't find that big fucker Big Boy, so they just trashed the place. No significant damage, just broken glass and shit like that." He still wore a frown. "They were gone by the time we showed up. It's a good thing too because we're running out of places to hide these bodies you keep dropping."

Yeah, because it was my fucking fault. Whatever. "That all?"

"No." Cross stood closer, face as implacable as ever. "We're at a huge disadvantage here because this is our home turf, all of our shit is right here for them to fuck up."

Jag joined the circle and clapped a hand to my back.

"About that," I said without looking at him. "Rocky has a good plan that can help. If you're in, that is." Because I was done asking. Either they would help, or they wouldn't.

"A plan? If she can plan this shit, why can't she just do what the fuck he wants?" Savior growled, glaring at Rocky.

"The same reason you tried to protect Mandy from Roadkill, asshole. You know what, forget it. Let's go, Rocky."

"Fuck," Cross growled behind me. "Fine, let's hear it. Not here though."

I held Rocky's hand and followed my brothers down the dimly lit back hall and out into the night air. It was cooler now with a slight breeze but none of that seemed to matter in the moment.

"Rocky can explain it better than I can." She glared at me and I gave her an encouraging nod and placed my hand on her hip.

"Fine."

She gave them the basics as we had discussed on the drive down, but she failed to mention that she'd already reached out. "He'll come unhinged and act rash. If we're lucky he'll start shit with someone else and they can take care of him for us, but I don't believe I have that much luck so it's just a first step."

## Wonderfully Wrecked

Savior was the first to respond with a long, low whistle. "Fuck me little girl, that's a damn good plan." He winked at Rocky who kept a careful, blank expression on her face.

"We might even be able to make some cash on this too, a few stacks just for intel. Think about it."

"Maybe, but I don't like it." Cross protested.

"Because it wasn't your idea," Rocky shot back defensively.

"No, because I have more than you and your kid to fucking think about! Shit!"

To her credit, Rocky didn't even flinch at his outburst. She nodded and pulled her phone from her pocket, staring at the screen like it held the secrets of the universe.

"I'll let you know what I decide."

Cross glanced at each of us but Rocky never looked up or acknowledged him.

"I'm out of here." She brushed past me and Jag, marching toward the parking lot in sharp, angry strides. I didn't blame her, but she wasn't going anywhere. Not tonight.

"Rocky, please. Be reasonable."

She turned, hair wild and unkempt just like her eyes. "I am being reasonable! I didn't want to come here and beg for their help, *you* did. You may have to follow his orders but I don't and I won't."

"Fine. Stay here tonight, with me and tomorrow I'll figure something else out, okay?" She stared at me, eyes rightfully suspicious at my easy surrender. "Don't make me carry you, Rocky. On second thought, make me."

"Ugh, you are infuriating, Lasso!" She pushed at my chest and pounded her little fists against me until she grew tired. Exhausted. Wobbly. Too wobbly. And then her legs were giving out while my heart raced, and my arms reached out grab her.

"Hey, take it easy sweetheart. Don't get so worked up."

"I'm fine," she said, trying to push out of my grasp. But I held on tight.

"It's past time for my next meal and this little guy gets cranky when I skip meal time."

"Guy? Do you know something, is it a boy?"

I didn't care, not really, as long as the baby was healthy. But the idea of having a son did something to me.

"You were at the last appointment. Lasso. You know what I know."

She pushed at my chest again and this time I stepped back.

"Can you show me where I'm sleeping tonight?"

"Don't you want to eat first?" The woman loved food, relished it more than any other woman I'd ever met. "You did almost pass out from hunger."

"Can you just bring me something up after you're done talking with your friends?"

Her gaze couldn't meet mine and I knew she was lying. She didn't want to spend any time with the guys who were my brothers. Not that I blamed her, but it didn't bode well for the future I was starting to see with her.

"Why don't you just eat down here with everyone and then go on up?"

"If you don't want to do it, just say so Lasso. I don't have time for this!"

Again she was marching off in no direction in particular, mumbling under her breath about, "useless fucking men."

"That one's gonna be a handful man, you sure you can handle her?" Jag stood beside me, tall and broad, with a smirk on his face.

"I sure as hell hope so since I went and married her."

It was as good a time as any to start telling people and Jag was my best friend.

"Holy shit, for real?"

"Yeah, but I don't think it matters. I get this feeling she's going to run. Rocky is a runner and she hasn't felt welcome around here so she's going to run. Scared and pregnant and alone."

"So make her stay."

"Just that easy?"

I didn't believe that for one fucking second. Rocky had been on her own for a long time and I didn't know if she was capable of leaning on another person, at least not when her life was in danger.

"Yep. If she wants to leave, go with her. If she wants to fight, let her yell and scream and then hug her and kiss her senseless. You might not get Cross to change his mind Lasso, but you have a decision to make, are you going to choose Rocky or listen to Cross?"

Sounded like two terrible fucking options to me but I got Jag's point loud and clear. "Yeah, thanks man."

"No problem. You need anything, call me."

The only thing I needed now was time and space to figure out what the hell I wanted beyond saving Rocky.

Rocky. That's what I wanted.

But first, we had to keep her alive.

# Chapter 19

*Rocky*

I never should have trusted Lasso to keep his word about leaving the Reckless Bastards compound. Not only was I still there three days later but I was restless as hell and damn sick of the tiny apartment they had us staying in until further notice. I was going crazy and today I would leave this damn property even if it killed me. Lasso was out with a couple of guys checking on their property to make sure nothing had been damaged overnight. This was the perfect time to go.

I slipped a paisley print dress over my head and tucked my feet into canvas shoes. My intention? To look like a girl just out and about, not a woman on the run in case anyone here gave a damn. I was pretty sure they didn't, but they'd promised Lasso to keep me safe and I suppose that meant something. To them.

To me, it meant my escape would be more difficult, but it didn't stop me from slinging a patchwork hobo bag over my shoulder and creeping down the metal steps in search of keys. Lasso was on his bike as were everyone but the women lingering around the place. And dammit! I saw at least a dozen sedans in the parking lot. I needed keys.

"Lookin' for something honey?" The guy had long black hair with a matching moustache that should have made him look creepy, but it didn't. Those grey eyes made him look like a wolf. A big, sexy, teasing wolf.

"Yeah, uh, dude. I'm looking for a set of car keys."

"Stitch, not dude. Please never call me dude from those sweet lips. Don't tell Lasso I said that." He winked, looking extremely boyish despite his manly appearance.

"Whatever. Keys?"

He shook his head. "No can do, babe. No one leaves without an escort."

Escort? Sounded exactly like the prison it felt like. I didn't like this, unable to move freely. It felt too much like my time with Genesis, which was how I got into this mess in the first place. I really needed to start making better decisions before I produced another generation of losers and quitters.

"Thanks for nothing, Stitch."

"Sorry, those are the rules."

I didn't give a damn about rules, especially someone else's fucking rules designed to keep me in check. I turned on my heels and stalked across the bar or whatever it was with pool tables, dart boards and other bar crap.

I pushed through the front doors, gasping as the sun hit my skin. I hadn't stepped outside in a few days and the heat felt invigorating and life-affirming after hanging out in the dark apartment for days on end.

But I could feel two sets of eyes on either side of me, courtesy of the goons at the door. "I know, I can't go anywhere. Ever. Got it."

"If you want to go out, come with me." It was Cross, the last person other than Genesis I wanted to go anywhere with, but beggars couldn't be choosers.

"Okay."

I followed him to a matte gray pickup truck and hopped in before he could attempt to help. We drove in silence and stopped along Mayhem's equivalent of Main Street where we both got out.

I followed him into an art supply store. I didn't really want to talk so I looked around, feeling more gratitude than I would ever admit when I realized I could buy supplies and paint in the shop.

"Excuse me," I said to the middle-aged clerk, "I notice palettes back there?"

"Yes, we have select paints and palettes if you want to paint by the hour." She named a very reasonable rate and I grinned my acceptance of the price, handing her the cash.

"I'm Moon, and this is my shop. You're new around here."

Was it written on my forehead? "I am. The name is Rocky. It's nice to meet you Moon, this is a great place."

# Wonderfully Wrecked

"You're an artist?"

I sensed a kindred spirit in this woman but maybe it was that we were dressed near identically except she had sunflowers instead of paisley.

"Not really but I have an online craft store ... which is temporarily down."

Shit, I'd managed to forget about that for a minute. Moon looked concerned and I shook it off.

"Never mind." I took my crap and set up at the end of the room, looking at the plate of food in the center to act as inspiration.

It was nice to just sit down and paint again, to get lost in the colors and textures of the Tomahawk steak, the red wine and the herb-flecked mashed potatoes. As I focused on the details the tension left my shoulders and as my mind finally cleared, the confusion lifted. Lasso was my husband now, no matter how or why it had come about, and that meant we were a team. I had to trust him and since he trusted his *brothers* I had to as well.

Even if they didn't like or trust me.

The painting complete, I sat back and smiled at the image. It wasn't all that creative, but the technique was good. I was about to ask Moon if she did regular classes, but she and Cross looked to be deep in conversation. That seemed weird, but I didn't care enough to question it. Except maybe to warn her away from the surly asshole. But that was none of my business. I took my painting outside and set it against the wall to dry while I enjoyed the feel of the sun on my skin.

The day was warm, and it had grown warmer since I'd been inside the art shop. It felt nice and it made me wish I were back home, in my apartment in San Diego. It was a five-minute walk from the beach and a walk along the sand always guaranteed to clear my mind. I realized I missed my old apartment and my old life.

My mind wandered this way and that. This was my first hour alone with nothing but time on my hands since Lasso and I had been on the run. I began to hear a motorcycle in the distance; as my ears pricked up it grew closer until the bike was on the sidewalk barreling right toward me. I jumped out of the way at the last minute, lost my footing and fell to the ground. A loud snap sounded but luckily it was just my phone on the concrete. And my sunglasses. Probably my e-reader too, dammit.

"Shit," I groaned, but when I tried to stand, a pain in my elbow radiated up to my neck.

"What in the hell do you think you're doing?"

When I focused my eyes, Cross was leaning over me, casting a long shadow that only made his scowl look more threatening. If I was inclined to feel threatened. Which I wasn't.

"Don't speak to her that way!" Moon snapped as she knelt beside me. Then she helped me up, carefully and tenderly. "Are you all right?"

"Other than the people trying to kill me and my baby, I'm fine. And I'm sorry to bring this trouble to your place, it's a great place."

A yelp of pain escaped when I straightened my arm.

"I'm fine," I lied, using my other arm to wipe concrete crud off me. I smiled at Moon but her dipped brows said she didn't believe me.

"Really."

She scowled at me but in a friendly way. "You're stubborn, I can tell but at least let me get you some ice for that elbow."

Without waiting for my agreement, she pulled me back inside and through to a back room where she sat me on a stool and wrapped ice in a tea towel.

"Lasso is going to fucking kill me," Cross complained as he raked both hands through his hair, a worried and slightly annoyed look on his face.

I sighed, trying not to hold it against him but he made it hard. "Too bad I moved so quickly, huh? You could have been rid of me permanently." He scowled and me; Moon gasped, glaring at him.

"Don't worry Moon, he doesn't like me but he's stuck with me for the moment so I'm safe."

"Let me help you to your car," she insisted, and I let her because it was nice to have someone fussing over me for no reason other than they were a good person.

"Thank you, Moon. If I make it through this, I'd love to come to a class." I hugged her in an odd show of sentimentality before using my good arm to propel myself into the truck.

"Goodbye, Rocky. Cross," she said with a hint of censure when she said his name before walking away, leaving a melody of clashing bangles in her wake.

"I don't dislike you," Cross said with a hint of annoyance. "I'm just worried about my friend."

There was no point even trying to reply to that. No matter how many times I told him that I didn't want Lasso hurt any more than he did, he wouldn't believe me. So I was done defending myself.

"Then don't tell him it happened. It doesn't matter anyway."

"Is that how you live your life, keeping secrets?" He sounded so disdainful and disgusted I wanted to jump out of the car just to get away from him.

"There's no one in my life to keep secrets from. It's just me." It used to be just me.

"Not anymore."

"We'll see about that," I told him because I was pretty sure that this would all end just how I thought it would. Badly.

My gaze stayed on the blurry asphalt as we zoomed back to the compound and when we arrived in the parking lot I muttered a rushed, "Thanks," and made my way to the tiny apartment that was my temporary home. I climbed the stairs, undressed on my way to the bed and curled up under the blankets where I let myself cry until my eyes ran dry.

And I stayed there for the next four days.

# Chapter 20

*Lasso*

"She hasn't left the apartment in five days and I don't know what in the hell to do about it."

Jag and I were inside my house again, assessing the damage left by Genesis' thugs and looking for any clues we could find.

"She won't talk, only eats enough to keep from being sick and she cries all the damn time, man. She thinks I can't hear it."

Jag's eyebrows rose. "In that shoebox?"

"Right? She hides it behind the shower, the toilet, cooking or anything else she can find to hide the sound of her tears. What the fuck?"

Jag shrugged, pensive as always while he looked around the place.

"Put yourself in her position, Lasso. She's stuck with a bunch of strangers who made it no secret they don't trust her, pregnant and married to a man she doesn't know *and* who doesn't love her. I'm stressed and it's not my life."

He made a good point and I nodded, going to the back of the house to check things out. "They got in through here, cut out one window on the door." They'd just smashed shit up, probably in anger or maybe just because they could.

"You hear that?" Jag put two fingers to his lips and pointed to the front where I heard a car door shut. "Stay here, I'll cover the front entrance."

I nodded and watched him go, my heart racing as I waited. And waited.

The doorbell rang and I held my breath until it became clear these assholes were bold as fuck. I joined Jag just as the door opened to reveal two assholes, one black and one white, both of them with Killer Aces on their jackets.

"We don't want any," I said.

"Good, because we ain't selling asshole."

## Wonderfully Wrecked

Jag was alert and I smirked. "Then what the fuck are you doing on my doorstep?" I took a step up and sized up each of those motherfuckers, looking for weaknesses. They were both strapped on the right side but the white one wore his watch on his right hand. Big muscles, but they weren't smart. Fucking amateurs.

"We're looking for a friend, Big Boy. Know where we can find him?"

"Big ass black dude with a huge smile? Nope, haven't seen him." Jag snickered, and the guy lunged but caught my fist in his throat. "I don't think so, motherfucker."

"I'm. Gonna. Kill. You." He was doubled over with his hands at his neck. I just laughed.

"Calm down, Wheezy," I said. "Tell us what the fuck you want!"

The other one lunged again but Jag was ready for his ass with a knee to the gut so when the asshole bent forward, Jag wrapped his arm around his throat and squeezed.

"My brother asked you a question. Answer and you get to keep breathing." When he needed to be, Jag was a stone-cold asshole. People never saw it coming but it was always a fucking treat to watch. He squeezed tighter to prove his point and the gasping began.

I drew back my fist and let it go straight at the dude's nose. It was hard enough to hurt like hell, but it wasn't broken and when he went down my foot went to his throat.

"Okay, you assholes want to do this the hard way? I'm game. It's been awhile, hasn't it Jag?"

"Too damn long." His eyes were as wide as his smile, making Jag look crazy as fuck. "So."

Wheezy said, "Just give us the fucking girl, man. She ain't worth all this." He tapped my boot and I eased up. A bit.

"Tell that to your crazy ass friend Genesis, because Rocky is mine and I ain't giving her up." I pressed again until he choked and groaned, smacking at my leg. "Got me?"

"Then this is gonna get messy," the other one said, gasping for air under Jag's arm.

"It's a good thing we like it messy." Then before I took another breath I screamed, "Fuck!"

That asshole punched me in the dick and I bent over before I could stop myself, catching his fist on the way down. "Goddammit!"

The fucker lunged at me and I moved, landing a blow to the side of his head, then again with both hands as he took me down.

"Or," he grunted, "I could just kill you right now, kill your friend and go get that bitch before any of my boys get hurt."

"Too late for that, dick breath." I hated assholes like him who talked too much. But it gave me plenty of time to grab the blade from my pocket and stick it in his gut, deep enough to hurt but not do real damage.

"Call her a bitch again so I can twist this fucker in your fat gut. Go on, do it." He gasped and clenched my wrist to stop me from making good on my promise, but I held on tight. "Tell your boss he won't survive this."

"He won't care," he gasped.

I let go and rolled away before he fell on top of me. "Next time I see you, I'll kill you."

Jag squeezed the guy's neck until he was on the verge of passing out, then he let go. "That goes double for me. Now get the fuck outta here!"

They struggled to help each other to their feet and ran off while Jag and I watched with shit-eating grins. And a hint of a grimace on my part. How in the fuck they planned to ride bikes with those injuries I didn't know. Then again, I didn't really give a shit either. "Damn that was fun."

Jag looked at me and grinned. "Come on, Lasso. You are one crazy motherfucker." We went back inside, and I grabbed a few things for me and Rocky. The rest of it would have to wait until this shit with Genesis was over, when I could get a cleaning crew in here without risking their safety.

## Wonderfully Wrecked

"That's it for now," I told him and we both headed for the front door just as my land line began to ring.

Jag gave me a look like I was a dumb shit. "Dude, you still have a fucking land line? What are you, fifty?"

"Asshole," I grumbled and picked up the phone. "What?"

"Let's be reasonable, man. I have the power to destroy your little club, and I will if Rochelle doesn't come back and help me."

I barked out a laugh. "Power? You? I have a deal for you Genesis, forget about Rocky, go the fuck away and I won't have to kill you."

He might have thought he was big shit, but he was fucking with the wrong man and the wrong damn club.

"Not if I get to you first."

Another laugh escaped me. "Don't count on it, asshole." I hung up the phone, satisfied as fuck that I could slam it hard enough to crack the damn thing.

"What are we gonna do?"

"We head back and hope like hell Rocky's plan will bear some fruit."

"That's a lot of hope."

"At the moment, it's all we got."

\*\*\*

Rocky was snuggled up in my arms, sleeping soundly with a satisfied smile on her face. After the run-in with the Genesis assholes yesterday, I came back and found her still sad but no longer crying. She took one look at me, drew me a hot bath, washed me, sucked me dry and then fucked me until all I could do was curl around her and sleep.

On and off for the past twenty-four hours, she couldn't get enough of me. We lost ourselves in sweet, hot fucking. It was soft and slow, hungry and intense, it was everything and then some. Too bad she hadn't said anything more than a few dirty phrases the entire time.

## Wonderfully Wrecked

Her cellphone rang and I nudged her awake and took a quick look at the clock. Two seventeen in the fucking morning. That couldn't be good. "Rocky, babe, your phone."

She groaned, half turning and blindly reaching for it. "Yeah?"

"You fucking bitch!"

The stupid son of a bitch shouted so loud it was like he was in the damn room with us. "I fucking know you had something to do with this shit!" Genesis was seething, I could hear him foaming at the mouth even over the phone.

Rocky's lips curled into a smile. "Something to do with what, Genesis?"

"Don't you fucking play dumb with me, you stupid bitch! When I get my hands on you Rochelle, I'm gonna make you pay."

"Interesting word choice," she murmured, stretching and drawing my eyes to creamy, naked tits. "Did you have a reason for calling?"

"My goddamn stash houses, Rochelle! I don't know how but I know you had something to do with this shit and I promise you'll pay. Maybe I'll finally get a pretty dollar for selling that sweet ass of yours. I know some real sick fucks who'd pay good money to fuck you up, princess."

I reached for the phone then, prepared to reach through that motherfucker and choke the life from him but Rocky leaned away from me. "How on earth would a stupid bitch like me know anything about stash houses, whatever *that* is."

"Too much," I mouthed to her and she rolled her eyes.

"It's funny now, but after I fucking kill your punk-ass boyfriend, you'll have no one to protect you."

She sat up and pushed her hair from her eyes with her free hand. "Husband, actually. Lasso is my husband, Genesis." She stunned him into silence. "What, no words of congratulations?"

"Too bad you'll be a widow soon." He spat out the words, but Rocky was tough as nails. She didn't even flinch. "Unless you give me a couple weeks. Remember how kind I was to you?"

"I remember your brand of kindness, Genesis. And I've moved on from it. Now maybe if you stop this shit right now, you might not lose everything." Her threat was clear, if not explicit.

"Rochelle be reasonable. It's just a couple jobs that you can plan in your sleep."

"Are you really begging me? Maybe you should have fucking asked nicely instead of threatening me, fucking up my property and threatening my friends! Now, Genesis, now I say fuck you! And I'm going to make sure everything you love burns to the fucking ground!"

She ended the call and tossed the phone across the bed. Her hands were shaking and tears streamed down her cheeks.

Fucking goddamn tears. They wrecked me every fucking time. "You handled him perfectly, Rocky."

"Yeah, I know, but these pregnancy hormones don't play around. The baby doesn't like to be stressed or angry."

I stood to get her something to drink when there was a knock at the door.

I ran to the door, knowing good news doesn't come calling at three in the morning.

"Jag, what's up?" His expression was serious as fuck, sober and stone cold.

"There was a break-in at Bungalow Three," he said referring to one of the whorehouses the club owned. "They slapped around a few of the girls but when more guys arrived, they began shooting. A few guys are injured but those fuckers are locked in with the girls. Backup is needed."

Rocky appeared at my side, wrapped in a silky, flowered robe. "Sorry about all this," she told Jag.

"Don't apologize for that, ever. Just keep my godchild safe in there, yeah?"

She smiled sheepishly and nodded. "I'm doing my best." Rocky turned to me and cupped one side of my face, green eyes shining with worry and affection. "Don't worry about me, a few words will only piss me off. Stay safe, Lasso." She patted her belly. "This little guy and me? We're counting on you."

I turned my face into her hand and pressed a kiss to her palm. "I'll keep you safe."

"I know. You guys be safe and I'll place a few more calls to fulfill my promise to my ex."

I grinned and left with Jag, smiling as I thought about how fucking tough Rocky was. Tougher than even she realized. I gave Jag a quick rundown of the phone call with Genesis and his eyes bugged out of his head.

"Cross'll be pissed that you disobeyed him."

We hopped on our bikes. "He can be pissed all he wants. She made the first round of calls on our way back from Idaho." Jag smiled, started his bike and we made our way to Bungalow Three. From the outside it looked like a big ass tiki hut, complete with thatched fucking roof in the middle of the desert. We slowed near the entrance, pulling our bikes up near the others at the wooden gate.

Cross was waiting when we hopped off.

"Did you check that shit over there?" I asked. "A few Roadkill vests mixed in with the Killer Aces."

"Yeah I saw it," he grumbled and rubbed a hand over his face, calculating how much damage we could do with the guys already here against at least a dozen that we could see.

Stitch sauntered over with a deadly serious expression on his face. "I got some semi-autos in the back of the truck, Prez." With an ortho boot on his ankle from a bar fight, Stitch jerked his thumb at his antique Chevy, his smile as shiny as new fucking tires. "Want me to get'em?"

# Wonderfully Wrecked

"Fuck yeah," Cross nodded, scanning the area around the building in search of more backup.

Stitch howled with glee. "Let's fuck up some shit, boys!" He limped his tall ass to the Chevy and lifted the southwest print blanket in back to reveal a dozen automatic weapons.

"Can't take the redneck out of the biker, that's for fucking sure," Jag joked, smacking Stitch on the back. "I think your math is off man, there are only five of us."

He picked up two, strapping one over each shoulder.

"Two for me since I got a gimp leg," Stitch said, "the rest of you fuckers take what you can handle."

Savior grabbed two and handed the rest over to us, staring at each of us until everyone was silent with their eyes on him. "Jag and Stitch, you stay out here and pick'em off as they exit. Careful of the girls. Golden Boy will go around back with me. Max, Cross and Lasso will go through the front. Eyes alert boys, kill any *kutte* that's not our own and meet up by Stitch's ugly ass truck."

"Fuck you," he said, smiling wide with one gun perched on his shoulder.

We broke apart and executed orders perfectly with me bringing up the rear. We entered the house, checking every fucking room. Left room, clear. Right, clear each of us yelled out as we cleared the rooms, mostly of naked hookers just trying to earn a living in the middle of this shit show.

"Clear," Max called out behind me just as a Killer Ace stepped into the hall six feet from me. My gun went up and I squeezed the trigger in two tight bursts, dropping that asshole to the ground.

"Clear," I yelled back to the sound of Savior chuckling. "Head outside to Jag," I told the girls because they all loved his quiet ass. We headed to the second floor, performing the same actions but this time I could hear the heavy footfalls of motorcycle boots.

## Wonderfully Wrecked

A scream sounded to my left and I kicked the door in and ducked, missing a spray of bullets but returning fire, hitting a Roadkill member in the leg. "Shit!"

"Go find Jag," I yelled to two more girls in nothing but lacy panties and panicked glances as they ran by. Max moved ahead of me, his big body blocking my view.

Another girl tried to run past, but the hall was too narrow and she paused, big blue eyes looking tired and terrified. "There are three guys in the suite at the end of the hall with two of our newbies."

"Thanks sweetheart. Jag is waiting out front. Be careful and take any other women you see with you." I looked down and noticed the blade clutched in her hand. "Use it on anyone who's not a Reckless Bastard."

"Damn straight," she said and took off at a run with no apparent thought to her naked tits and bare feet.

Max kicked the door open and let off two shots, taking out a Killer Ace, leaving me and Cross to handle the other two. Cross sent his man to his knees with a shot in the gut while I hit a Roadkill member right through his fucking Adam's apple.

"Well that was easy as fuck," Max joked, winking at the scared young women.

"It's all right ladies, go downstairs and wait for us." I helped each one up and sent them out the door so we could clear the rest of the building.

"Yo!" Cross whistled and me and Max both went running, finding Alana with a Killer Ace wrapped around her throat. Her brown eyes were frantic, scanning the room, probably wondering if this would be the last thing she ever saw. At thirty-two, she was older than all the other girls and she did the books and bookkeeping for the club, which meant she was doubly club property.

I stepped forward. "Hey, Alana, how you doing sweetheart?"

"I've been b-b-b-better, Lasso."

"I know it, but you look good," I told her and she blushed.

"Give me the bitch I want," the Killer Ace shouted, letting spittle fly every fucking where. "And you can have this one and all the rest."

Cross laughed. "Look around man, what others? Our girls are safe and all your boys are dead or hurt."

And now that wild look entered the eyes of the Killer Ace, the look of all cornered animals. The smart ones figure out how to live to fight another day, the dumb ones charge forward without thinking. Anxious to strike.

"Just let her go," he said with some stupid kind of bravado. Did he even know it was going to get him killed?

"That's not happening," I told him as Cross and then Max raised their guns, aimed at his head. "Do you really want to die because Genesis can't take rejection? Several of his stash houses have been hit. Can he even pay you to cover your medical bills if you get shot?"

"How about if you get a good ass whoopin'?" Max asked with a menacing laugh.

The fucker barked out a laugh and squeezed around Alana's neck. "Can this bitch? You should be thinking about this hot property right here instead of the boss's old piece of ass because he's getting that bitch."

This piece of shit should have been more careful because he fell right into our trap. "That sounds like bullshit from where I'm standing," I told him.

"Sounds like somebody is writing a check his ass can't cash," Cross tossed out, forcing his attention to dart between us. His finger slipped from the trigger and I turned to Alana.

"Hey Alana, remember that story I told you about my old horse, Baby?" She nodded almost imperceptibly, eyes wide and alert. "Do for me what I forgot to," I told her and when she hit the ground, I lit that motherfucker up like I was Bruce Willis in *any* fucking movie *ever*.

The room fell silent for several long moments and then Alana's bloodcurdling scream pulled us from our thoughts. The fucker had fallen right on top of her and Max was there, tossing his big ass off Alana.

It took nearly an hour before the place was completely clear and we had the bodies of two Roadkill and three Killer Aces.

"Five got away," Savior grumbled when we and Golden Boy returned to the group. "Through the woods."

"I think I clipped one of 'em," Golden Boy said, hands on his knees as he sucked in air.

"Stitch and I are going back to the clubhouse. Someone needs to pick up Doc. A few of the girls have wounds."

Jag had his arms wrapped around two of the girls, leading them to the Chevy with the kind of tenderness they needed.

"Roadkill and Killer Aces together. How the fuck did that happen?" I looked to Cross to see if he had any insight.

"The same way you and that girl reached out to his enemies, he went after ours. Though after what we did to those fuckers, I'm not surprised." None of us said it, but we all knew we weren't done with the war yet.

Once we dealt with the Killer Aces, we'd have to deal with the Roadkill motherfuckers.

## Chapter 21

*Rocky*

If Lasso thought I'd fall back to sleep once he and Jag left to kick some ass and shoot some outlaws, he was sorely mistaken. I'd spent the whole night pacing, hoping none of the women were hurt because of me, and then the baby began to toss and turn, causing me discomfort and nausea so I sat down like a good little mama.

And I began to knit.

It wasn't much, just a cotton rainbow thread that would become a baby beanie, but it was more than enough to keep my mind off what Lasso was doing. And why. I'd placed those other calls, giving away four more stash house locations and hoped it would force Genesis to make a mistake. He was already on the edge; that phone call earlier proved it. One more little nudge from me would be the thing that tipped him over.

I must have dozed off for a while because a knock on the door woke me and Lasso wouldn't knock.

I grabbed the gun he'd left. I stood with my stomach facing away from the door as I peeked through a small opening. A curvy blonde stood on the other side. She looked harmless so I opened the door.

"Hi, I'm Jana, Max's wife. I just wanted to check on you. May I come in?"

Max at least seemed sorry about not helping so I said, "Sure. Did you draw the short straw to come up here?" Lasso had been a tad overprotective lately, so it wouldn't surprise me if he'd forced her up here.

"No, but I know what it's like to be new around here and how intimidating it can be."

Arm crossed defensively, I jutted my chin out. "I'm not intimidated. They don't want me here and I don't want to be either. I came to Lasso, not the club."

She laughed, and the sound was soft and low. "All this comes with the territory, but it's not so bad." Jana did seem happy, but she was also in love and had planned and married her guy on purpose.

"Are you really all right? This has to be tough, Rocky. And you haven't come down all week. Are you even eating?"

I sighed, trying to be nice because this woman was making an effort. "Lasso is force feeding me daily."

"Good," she grinned. "Max was the same, feeding me all the time, forcing water down my throat, taking bags of groceries from of my arms and forcing me to sit. It was annoying but nice."

"Yeah well, I'm used to taking care of myself."

"So am I," she snorted and pointed to the scar on her face.

"It's hardly even noticeable with how pushy you are."

She laughed and seemed not offended in the slightest. "Thanks. Do you have a birthing plan yet?"

I shook my head and she rattled off about a dozen different things I needed to do before the baby arrived. The list was daunting, and my knitting hands stopped, taking in the gravity of my future. If there was a future.

"It seems like a lot but lucky for you, Teddy and I both have recently had babies."

"Must be something in the water," I grumbled, pulling another laugh from her.

"It's those big sexy bikers and you know it." She winked and leaned back, staring at me. "This will be easier if you make some friends, build a support system."

"Like I said, I'm used to taking care of things myself."

"I know, so was I. But when it comes to your kid you'll do whatever you have to, including digging in roots. Becoming part of a community."

That sounded nice, like all of the things I used to want for myself. Friends to do things with, like go to happy hour, share retail therapy binges, movie marathons and bitching sessions about relationships. I'd always wanted that but with every year that passed it became more apparent that I would not get it. Eventually, I stopped wishing. Then I stopped thinking about it altogether.

"I doubt I'll be sticking around once this is all over."

"That's too bad. Max says you and Lasso seem like the real deal, even if you guys can't see it yet." The emphasis she put on 'yet' set me on edge but I had a feeling that was her intent.

"It's not like that." And even if things were like that with Lasso and me, there was no way his so-called brothers would ever accept me. "There's too much baggage, even if it was a possibility. Which it isn't."

"Why isn't it? Clearly there's something between you, besides a baby, or Lasso wouldn't look ready to castrate the world to keep you safe."

That was bullshit. "You have a kid, so you already know the lengths a man will go to protect his child. The only difference is that you guys are in love so you see it differently." I realized how bitchy that sounded and groaned. "Look, I'm not trying to be mean but there is no me and Lasso. If I hadn't tracked him down, we would've never seen each other again."

"But you did. And now you're married and having a baby. I think you're underestimating Lasso's feelings."

Maybe I was. "Still, it doesn't matter. His *brothers* don't trust me, and I don't trust them either. When this is all over, no one will be able to forget that." Least of all me. "I appreciate your advice but we both know when it comes to this club, nothing compares."

It looked like Jana had finally gotten the hint. As much as I appreciated her attempt to help, my situation was unique and I would handle it myself. She gave a resigned sigh and turned her disappointed shoulders toward the door. "If you need anything or you just want to talk, give me a call."

"Thank you, Jana. I mean it."

## Wonderfully Wrecked

She nodded and looked at me with sad green eyes. "Lasso is a really good guy and no matter what happens between the two of you, he deserves a chance to watch his kid grow up."

"I know," I grumbled and went back to the sofa after she left. It was the part that left me struggling too. I couldn't deprive our child of knowing a father like Lasso and I couldn't deny him the chance at being the father he was destined to be.

Which meant I might have to stay in Vegas. Plant roots.

Settled in.

My phone rang and I snatched it up, hoping it was Lasso to tell me everything was done and done. Over. Everyone safe. "Hello?" I should have looked at the screen.

"Rochelle. Meet me at the southwest end of the property in thirty minutes."

"Forty," I countered.

"Don't make me wait a minute more. I'm not in a forgiving mood, Rochelle." He ended the call and I took several deep breaths, calming my racing heart and emptying my mind.

Then I sprang into action.

# Chapter 22

*Lasso*

When I got back from Bungalow Three all I wanted was Rocky and a shower, not necessarily in that order. But when I got to the apartment upstairs, it was empty. With all the shit that had already gone down, my first instinct was to panic but Genesis had already put in his harassing call for the day. Still, I turned and went back down the stairs and into the clubhouse. I checked the bedrooms in back as well as the common area, but she was nowhere to be found.

Now, I was fucking panicked.

I went back upstairs to our apartment because I knew if she'd left here of her own free will, she would have left some kind of clue.

And I hoped like hell she did.

I sagged in relief when I saw her hand-drawn plans of the whole Reckless Bastards compound. At least the parts she could see and learn about from others. It was laid out with three pennies taped to it, each one wrapped in a different color yarn. My lips quirked in a smile at the fact she'd used the same yarn from the baby beanie for whatever this map was meant to be. Since I didn't know, I needed help.

I found Jag and Cross out in back sharing a joint. "What's up?" Jag was my best friend and knew me better than anyone. He took one look at me and was immediately on alert.

"Rocky isn't here. No signs of a struggle but she's gone. Left this." I laid out the hand drawn plans and took a step back, hoping some of it meant something to someone else.

"Where in the hell did she get such detailed plans?" Cross was angry. Tired and angry weren't a good mix with him, but I was worried about my pregnant wife. His feelings would have to wait.

"She drew them from memory so she could be prepared if she needed to make a fast getaway."

Jag grinned. "What a woman."

"Yeah. See anything helpful?"

Jag looked at the plans for a few minutes, taking in every detail before he honed in on a set of numbers in one corner. "I think we got something." He pointed again and stood with that excited look he got when a digital mystery was in front of him.

"What the fuck is that supposed to be? It's nonsense," Cross insisted angrily, taking a long pull off the joint and blowing the smoke toward the sky. "Maybe she decided to end this without more bloodshed."

"That would solve all your problems wouldn't it?" He glared at me, ready to tell me off I was sure, but Jag had left and come back with one of his laptops, started it up and plugged the numbers into some program.

"Damn." Jag smiled at the screen then looked up at me and Cross. "She's damn smart. Those numbers allow me to access her phone, her microphone and GPS." His fingers flew over the keyboard as he spoke.

"We can track her in real time, which means we can get to her before whatever this plan is, pans out. Got her."

My phone rang as my gaze focused on the red dot and I absently hit the speaker button. "Rocky, what the fuck, babe?"

"I'm sorry, Lasso but I had to do it this way. I couldn't risk anyone else getting hurt. Are the girls all right?"

She sounded small and worried and I hated that. Rocky was at her best when she was strong and vibrant and lively.

"They're fine, Rocky. Come back here now, please."

She sighed. "I can't, not yet. This won't end any other way Lasso, you know it, too. Genesis wants to meet and I'm about five minutes away from the meeting spot but knowing him it's more like three. Did Jag get the data I left?"

"We got it, Rocky. Just keep your phone unlocked."

## Wonderfully Wrecked

"Already done. You'll be able to hear everything. I won't be able to hear you, so I'll say anything else you need to know. I sketched out a quick plan on the other side of those blueprints. It's short but if you can get into position in eight minutes it just might work."

Jag was already flipping over the plans, but my mind was racing. "What plans? Fuck!"

"Sorry Lasso but I couldn't let you talk me out of this. Be mad when this is over. Baby and I need you focused." She was right dammit but that didn't mean I had to like it, listening as she entered the fucking lion's den on purpose. "I gotta go." She ended the call.

I turned to Jag. "Tell me this is gonna work."

He nodded, sketching out a few things next to Rocky's notes. "Yeah, it's gonna work but we need three more men. At least."

"I'll get'em," Cross said easily, shocking the hell out of me.

"How about one fucker big enough for three?" Savior nudged between me and Cross, bringing with him an unexpected arrival.

"Gunnar! Man, shit! How the fuck are you?" I couldn't hide my happiness that our VP was back. Gunnar was funny and fair, a shit starter with a soft spot for damsels in distress. I was as close to him as I was to Jag but he'd been dealing with the death of his mother and some other personal things lately. Now that he was back, I couldn't deny my pleasure at his timing.

"I could be better, brother and once we get your girl back, we can drink all about it." He grinned and turned so we could see the chubby ball of black hair and blue eyes in his arms. "For now, say hi to Maisie. My sister."

I blinked at his confession, but I couldn't help but smile at the little drooling bundle. "Well, shit, I guess we do have plenty to drink about."

"Okay guys listen up," Jag called out. "We now have six and half minutes to get into position." He handed out comms as he spoke. "She chose an outdoor location at the southwest side of the property where those small hangars still stand." He rattled off all the notes Rocky had left about how many men she expected Genesis to bring with him, their types of guns and shooting ability.

Savior stepped forward with a smile at the same time Stitch came out with vests for us all. "Not that I don't trust Rocky, but I think it's better to go in over-armed. A lot can change in a couple years."

He was right, then again Savior was the Sergeant at Arms and he knew his weapons. "A couple of the prospects are bringing out shit. Take what you need fast and let's get the fuck going."

That was Savior, short and sweet when he needed to be.

"I'll get Rocky," I told Savior, my eyes serious. My demeanor didn't allow any fucking argument.

"That's fine. I'll kill a motherfucker who gets off on threatening pregnant chicks."

God, I fucking loved my club.

# Wonderfully Wrecked

# Chapter 23

*Rocky*

Nerves. They were a son of a bitch, wreaking havoc with my ability to think logically or breathe normally. I could hear noise in the distance, the hum of a motor and footsteps on gravel. Genesis, the bastard. Of course he hadn't come alone. I didn't expect he would, which is why I took the extra time to ensure my safety as much as I could when dealing with a raging fucking lunatic.

To make matters more intense, I had no idea if my cavalry would be Lasso and Jag or an actual cavalry of men who would kick ass, shoot bullets and make Genesis and his Killer fucking Aces regret they'd crossed the border into Nevada. I had no idea and I wouldn't until it was too late, so I really hope I didn't misplace my trust.

"Rochelle, looking good. A little fat for my tastes, but good."

# Wonderfully Wrecked

His voice came from straight ahead and I stopped, looking up to see where he was. It was difficult to see because his SUV lights were shining bright. "Wish I could say the same."

"Had to make sure you listened this time. I know listening has always been difficult for you." His sickening sneer made me wish I'd come with something other than a small gun strapped to my thigh.

"I listen just fine Genesis, I just don't always want to do what you want me to."

He laughed that sickeningly soft chuckle he used when he wasn't really amused. "Because you always think you know best. Now look at where we are." Genesis shook his head as he stuck his hand inside the car and turned off the high beams. He hadn't changed. Same shaggy copper hair brushing his shoulders, same pouty mouth more suitable to a male model than a gangster. I couldn't see his smoky gray eyes, but I'd bet they were bloodshot with a combination of pills and coke.

"Where exactly are we?" I crossed my arms and looked off to his side because I knew it would rile him. I needed him wild and reckless and I could push until he flashed a handgun.

"Goddammit, Rochelle stop playing these fucking mind games!" His arms jerked forward, and he kicked a leg out sideways in a show of temper, but a quick pinch to the bridge of his nose and Genesis was calm again. Sort of. "Look, just come with me now and work with me until I'm satisfied I've been paid back for all the pain and suffering you've caused me, then you can come back here and play house with that fucking cowboy."

I smiled at his disdain for Lasso. He never did like men who were too good looking, said he couldn't trust them but the truth was he couldn't stand the jealousy. "I'm not going anywhere with you Genesis."

"Come on," he cajoled softly, grinning with that little head tilt he thought made him look hot but really he looked like Justin Bieber. "It's just a couple jobs. It could be like old times. I'll even think about keeping the brat around."

"Like I would ever want my kid around a headcase like you."

I shook my head, knowing I was poking the bear but unable to stop myself. He drew closer and I slowly drew back, reaching around my waist for the gun. "How about this Genesis? You go home and you might make it back in time to save another stash house or two."

He took two steps forward and then lunged, pulling back his hand and punching me in the nose before I could move. "You still got a smart fuckin' mouth. I always hated that about you."

I fell to my knees; grateful he didn't break my fucking nose. I looked up at him with a smile. "How many of your safe houses have been hit, Genesis? Two? Four? Seven?"

"Laugh it up, Rochelle. It'll probably be the last time you laugh for a long time." He smiled, pacing back and forth in front of me. "I have shit you know nothing about so don't think you can ever hurt me."

"You sure about that? Because I can remember at least a dozen, maybe more. In fact, a certain hazel-eyed gangster was very interested to learn about the house just off Pico."

Anger flashed again, and his foot raised high in the air, telling me exactly what he had planned. I rolled away and slid back on my ass, trying to stand without turning my back to him. "You're a dead bitch either way, Rochelle. The question is, do you want to live long enough for that bastard of yours to be born?"

I stood with a grunt. It wasn't elegant or intimidating but I wasn't foolish enough to believe I was either of those things. My heart raced. I could feel the baby projecting dissatisfaction with my mood but anything I did to draw attention would make my stomach a bigger target.

"I'm actually flattered, Genesis. To think that I mean more to you than all those stash houses. All that money. More than the new place in Santa Monica or that bungalow in West Hollywood right in the middle of all those families. Even more than that beauty salon with the hidden wall."

Jag had come through big time and the wide hazel eyes snarling back at me said I'd hit a nerve.

"I could just kill you now."

I nodded. "You could but after tonight you'll need me more than ever. Oh, and there's the fact that you're not getting out of here alive."

If Lasso didn't show up, I was more than prepared to make the easy choice if it came down to me and my baby or Genesis.

He laughed. "Your boyfriend is too busy worrying about his whores." He spat the word, waiting for my surprise or shock, maybe an emotional outburst.

"Oh, no!" I covered my head with one hand and my mouth with the other. "Was that what you were expecting? Sorry to steal your thunder but the women are fine. I'm not so sure your guys fared as well. And by the way, he's not my boyfriend. He put a ring on it." I flashed my ring finger, taunting him, digging my feet into the dirt to brace for the next blow.

Instead, he laughed. A quick glance at my wrist said I had two minutes before help arrived. With two large shapes behind Genesis' car, I hoped I called for enough men. Shit, I hoped enough men were allowed to come.

"I hope you had a good time on this little fucking vacation of yours, Rochelle, because you're mine. You. Are. Fucking. Mine. MINE!"

He reached for my arm and I jerked away from him, earning a backhand for my efforts.

"Yeah, you feel like a real big man now Genesis, smacking around a pregnant woman. I'm not yours, not ever."

"We'll see if you say that when I get rid of that fucking kid. I'll be doing the dumb son of a bitch a favor. With a dumb cunt like you for a ma, death is the best possible outcome." He shook his head. "I can't believe you were fucking stupid enough to come alone."

## Wonderfully Wrecked

Now it was my turn to laugh and I gave it the full maniacal, wide-eyed cackle. "Did you really think my husband would let his pregnant wife come alone to meet her unstable ex? You can't really be that stupid, can you?"

"I'll kill you, bitch!"

He lunged again but I wasn't quick enough to escape. His cool hand wrapped around my throat, leaving me to claw at his wrist and hand.

"It would be so easy to fucking end you right now you stupid fucking bitch. You're lucky I still need you."

I smiled, struggling for breath and thinking only of the oxygen my baby wasn't getting. "I'm a decoy to give him and his men time to fuck up your men and leave you all alone."

"Uh, fuck." He punched me again and let me fall to the ground, pulling his leg back to kick me, this time in the face. I blocked the worst of it but that left the baby unprotected and the next kick that came stole my breath.

"You motherfucker!" I reached for the gun, but it had fallen out of my hand and I scrambled to find it. "Better save your energy to ward off all those dicks you'll be taking up the ass in prison!"

*There it is!* I grabbed the handle and pulled it closer, ignoring the throbbing, spasming pain in my stomach.

His foot came up and he laughed, evil and joyful. "You wish. I won't kill you Rochelle. I'll kill that fucking bastard of yours instead." I squeezed the trigger twice, sending two bullets right into his stomach.

"Fucking. Bitch. Shot. Me." Big gray eyes stared at me, shocked as he dropped to his knees, both hands clutching his bleeding gut. "Rochelle."

He reached down to his side, but I was too mesmerized by the sight of the life flooding out of him to pay attention and then I heard it.

A loud pop.

But it was weird that I wasn't looking at Genesis anymore, but the night sky so black and velvety, sparkling with stars as a searing pain shot across the left side of my face, filling it with warmth. Two more shots sounded, at least I think so, but the ringing in my ears was too strong.

I smiled at the beautiful sky and then there he was, the man I'd been fighting for too long. The man I wanted more than I'd ever let myself admit. The only man since my dad that I ever loved.

"Lasso?" I waited for him to say something, anything. But he didn't.

Instead, everything went black.

# Chapter 24

*Lasso*

"How long does it take to get some fucking answers?" It felt like I'd been in this goddamn hospital waiting room for days, waiting for someone to come out here and tell me that Rocky was okay. Seeing that bastard kick her in the stomach and then watching her pass out in my arms took about fifteen years off my life. And now they wouldn't let me back there, wouldn't let me see her until they ran tests and treated her.

Bullshit.

I could have stayed at the clubhouse, but the guys had it handled and I saw the sheriff headed in as the ambulance took Rocky and me to the hospital. Everything was as clean as we needed it to be for the cops to show up. We'd made sure of it before even calling them.

The last I saw of Genesis, he was writhing in pain and begging for help. The fucking EMTs thought they would work on him first because he was bleeding, but I made them see the error of their ways. And now the universe was punishing me, making me sit here in silence with no information on Rocky.

She couldn't lose the baby. Not only would it take her from me, but it would break my heart. I'd gotten used to the idea of having a baby and being a dad. She'd been punched, kicked and shot tonight, put through the proverbial fucking ringer.

"Rochelle Izzo's family?"

I rushed to the doctor's side. "I'm her husband." It seemed like forever before he looked up from her chart to give me some news.

"Rochelle is mostly fine. The bullet graced her temple, so she'll have a scar. The baby is fine, his heartbeat is strong and other than an elevated blood pressure, there are no signs of distress." I stopped listening after a while, so relieved that she was going to be all right.

"Thanks, Doc. Can I see her?"

"Yes. She's been in and out of it since you brought her in, but she keeps mumbling *Dallas*."

I smiled. "That's me." It was damned pathetic to be so happy about something so little, but Rocky had a mile-wide independent streak so the fact that she was calling for me had to mean something.

It had to mean she felt something for me, I just knew it. But she was scared as hell, rightfully so, which meant it was up to me. And when I stepped inside that sterile, too-white fucking hospital room, with all the chirping, beeping and hissing, my eyes went to her. My heart skittered to a stop and kicked up again with a lot less energy.

Nothing had ever felt as good in my whole damn life as sitting in that hard orange plastic chair with her soft hand in mine. I rested my forehead on her thigh, my other hand on her belly, needing to touch her and see for myself that she was all right.

"You were so stupid. So fucking stupid and so incredibly brave. I wish you knew how tough you really are, even though I want to throttle you for going in there alone."

I pressed my lips to her palm, feeling relief settle over me when she squeezed back. "Now you just have to wake up so we can talk about the rest." All I wanted in that moment was for her to just open those big green eyes, long lashes framing them beautifully. That sight might get my heart beating normally again.

"The baby's okay?" Cross stood at the foot of the bed, looking nervous for the first time since I'd met him.

I nodded, my relief still palpable even an hour after receiving the news. "Yeah, Rocky took the brunt of it." I still couldn't believe she'd done that, curled around her belly to protect our kid. "They'll both be all right."

"That's good." I knew there was more so I just waited him out, not like I was leaving Rocky's side until she left this hospital. Maybe not even then. "Look Lasso, I owe you an apology. I had my reasons, but I never wanted anything to happen to her."

I stood and looked my Prez right in the eyes. "I know, man. No apology necessary. We had different ideas but in the end you came through, like I knew you would."

He barked out a laugh before catching himself and casting a sad glance at Rocky. "Make sure you tell that to your girl. I'm pretty sure she's never going to warm up to me."

"It'll take some time, but Rocky is pretty forgiving." It would be a long damn time before she warmed up to the club, but once I convinced her to stick around and stay married to me, she would. "Trust me."

"I do," he said in a tone more serious than our conversation warranted and I knew he meant something more. "Thought you might be hungry," he said and shoved a bag from the best damn taco place in all of Nevada into my hands.

I laughed and held up the bag. "You thought it would bribe Rocky, right?"

He shrugged. "Pregnant girls love food. I'm glad everything's okay."

"Me, too. Thanks, Cross."

"No problem."

He left and I ate four tacos before I slowed down. Finally, the excitement of the day took its toll. My head rested on Rocky's thigh, one hand holding hers and the other cupping her belly as I drifted off to sleep. They were safe. I didn't know how long I'd been asleep when I felt a hand brushing my hair. No, not brushing my hair, brushing past it.

"Damn tacos," she groaned and I smiled, lifting my head to look up at her, red hair standing in all directions and skin flushed from exertion.

"You're all right." I meant to just say it out loud to confirm but it ended up being a throaty groan. I stood and pressed my forehead to hers as relief settled in my bones. "You're all right." I said it again because it felt damn good after watching her pass out in my arms.

"I'm all right," she said on a shaky, teary sigh as she raked her fingers through my hair. "Really, Lasso, I'm fine. I mean, I lost the baby," she said on a sniffle, blinking like crazy to signal she was on the brink of tears. "So now we don't have to stay married and I'll have to start over. Again. But it's fine. I'm fine. See?"

I smiled and gave her a thorough once over. "You want to say fine one more time just to get it all out?"

It was slow, but she rewarded my patience with a soft, sad smile. "Fine. Now I said it for you so, you're welcome."

I gathered her hands in mine, kissing both sides of her hands, her fingers, letting the feel of her pulse racing against my lip settle my nerves.

"And you didn't lose the baby." I let that sink in because I knew it was what she was most worried about. "We didn't lose the baby."

"We … didn't?" Her hands went to her stomach and her eyes went to me for confirmation. "We didn't?"

## Wonderfully Wrecked

I shook my head and stood, pointing to the other monitor. "That's the baby's heartbeat right there. Strong like it should be. The kick hurt you more than the baby, but you both are fine, as long as you take it easy for a while. Let your husband take care of you."

"But that's—"

"Doctor's orders." She pouted but I could see the smile playing around her lips.

She leaned back but I noticed she didn't let go of my hand. "You don't have to, you know."

"I know Rocky, but dammit I want to. Seeing you take that bastard's beating and knowing I was too far away to do a damn thing about it tore me apart, but watching you pass out in my arms damn near killed me."

"I'm sorry I scared you. I had it under control, well, mostly." I leaned into her palm and closed my eyes, letting the sound of her breathing, the flowery scent of her skin wash over me.

"I'm just happy you both are all right." My lips brushed hers softly and I pulled back because I didn't want her mouth to distract me the way it all too easily did. "Rocky I don't want you to leave."

"I'm not going anywhere," she said as she gestured to the hospital bed. "Taking it easy, remember?"

I tried for a smile, but I couldn't because I knew what she was doing. It was exactly what I would have done before I met Rocky, created emotional distance with humor. "Not just now, Rocky. Forever."

She sucked in a breath, wide green eyes staring at me like I landed from another planet. "Lasso, don't. I don't need false promises."

"You know me better than that," I told her in a firm voice that held none of the anger I felt at her words. "You're already my wife and the mother of my child. Why would I lie now?"

"The baby," she said sadly.

"The baby is mine, too, whether you want to be with me or not. I'm talking about you. Us. I want this *us* to be permanent. You and me and the baby. Together."

"That's a tall order, cowboy."

"I'm a tall man, babe." She grinned. "Seriously, I don't know how else to tell you. I wish I had some pretty words to match your pretty face but all I have is me and the love I have for you in my heart. We've been through a lot in a really short time, more than most couples will go through in a lifetime and we're still here. Still wanting each other. Right?"

I hoped to hell that I hadn't misread all the signs that ran through my head in the ambulance ride to the hospital.

She nodded but Rocky was quiet. Too quiet.

"I love you Rocky. I know we got married for noble—but wrong—reasons. But now that you and the baby are safe, it's time to talk about us. I want us to stay married and raise that kid together, maybe even have a few more if you haven't created a craft store empire by then." I pressed a kiss to each of her palms and placed them over my chest. "That's what I want Rocky. You. Us. Everything."

"Okay," she said and swallowed nervously.

She should be nervous because what I had planned for her was a full onslaught of irresistible.

"You'll stay with me when they discharge you from here. You're free to stay in our room or the guest room. That should give you some time to take it easy and think about what you want from me, and from you. When you figure out what you want, or don't want, I'll be here."

She stared at me for a long time and I wondered what her green eyes saw, what she was taking in as she looked at my face. "You're really something Lasso, you know that?"

"Plenty of things are *somethin'* sweetheart."

She rolled her eyes and reached around my neck to pull me close.

"Something kind of special," she whispered against my mouth and then her lips were on mine. The kiss was slow and steady, both of us afraid that too much too soon would hurt her. I let her lead the kiss because she needed to and because nothing on God's green earth was better than Rocky writhing on me and moaning into my mouth.

"Thank you, Lasso. For understanding."

"No thanks necessary, sweetheart. I just need you to give us two things. Time and a real shot."

"See? Special," she said. "I can do that."

Then she kissed me again, this time she put all the words she wasn't ready to say to me yet into it.

That kiss, I knew, was the start of something special.

No, something better than special.

# Epilogue

*Rocky ~ One Month Later*

"Let me put that in your car for you." Moon was kind enough to let me spend the afternoon painting on the patio that connected her store to her backyard while she took care of inventory.

"I can handle it, Moon. You have plenty to keep you busy." She was a single mom with a sick child and she ran her own business. The last thing Moon needed was someone else to take care of. "Besides I still have to finish this sketch. My muse is starting to get restless."

"It's vewy hawd do sthay wike dis." Moon's adorable son Beau held his pose admirably even as he tried to talk around a protruding tongue.

"I told you to pick a pose you could hold for a long time." But like the burgeoning man he was, Beau did it anyway.

"Mom can I have a snack?"

"What's the rule?"

"Two good and one bad," he said like the world's most put upon kid before dashing into the blue house on the corner.

"I love your kid, Moon. How's he holding up?"

"Fine," she said and hoisted up the painting I'd finished. "More effective treatments become available everyday which means we're ... hopeful."

I followed Moon out to my car and hugged her when the painting was secure in the back seat. "I'll send good vibes into the world on his behalf. Thanks, and call if you need anything, even just an ear."

"Take care of yourself and stay off your feet the rest of the day," she ordered, like any good doula would.

I smiled and drove off, feeling cautiously happy about the friend I'd found in Moon this past month. It was fairly accidental since I couldn't do much of anything without risking the baby's life, but painting was another skill I could add to my repertoire to sell. I shouldn't have been surprised that she was a doula but when she made the offer it had floored me, seemed too hippy dippy with today's modern medicine. But Moon had a calming presence that helped, and Lasso had agreed so it all worked out.

In fact, Lasso had insisted because of the stress of the past few weeks. Genesis had been taken to the same hospital as me, where he spent four days in the ICU before succumbing to his injuries.

A deep sadness had enveloped me in the days following his death, not because I wanted him alive but because I was the reason he was dead. The cops hadn't agreed, calling it justified and sending me home with almost a thanks. Luckily, Big Boy had been released. A little battered and thinner than he'd ever been in his life, but he was grateful to be alive and promised Cross it was the last they'd see or hear from the Killer Aces. I couldn't believe they let him go but I was grateful. The last thing I needed was more bodies on my conscious while baking this baby.

Now I had to get home before Lasso did because I wanted to hang this painting as a surprise for him. If he really had gone to GET INK'D like he'd said, then he'd be home within the hour. However, I had feeling something else was going on. I'd heard him and the other Reckless Bastards talk about things like retaliation and Roadkill MC and I wondered what it was all about, though I trusted Lasso to tell me what I needed to know.

After a quick shower, I put steaks in the broiler and vegetables on top of the stove, along with potatoes because carb overload is the only good thing about being pregnant. Well, besides the baby at the end.

Lasso arrived about two hours later than expected, bloody and with torn clothing. I was on my feet as fast as I could, guiding him to one of the kitchen chairs. "Lasso, what the hell happened to you?" He sat with a groan and his head tilted back, giving me the perfect opportunity to scan for scars.

"Nothing much, just a fight with some assholes. Got sucker punched is all, but I'm okay, babe." He pulled me close, one big hand cupping my ass. "You look pretty as fuck today." His gaze wouldn't leave the sheer burgundy fabric covering my otherwise naked body.

"Thanks," I told him and pulled out of his grasp to get what I needed to clean up his split lip. "Even bloody you look good enough to eat," I told him with a sly smile.

He groaned when I grinned at his discomfort. "I'll be doing the eating tonight," he growled, hissing as I cleaned his lip.

"Maybe, but we should get you cleaned up first." I took his hand and pulled him to the upstairs bathroom that was big enough for two and I undressed him, letting my hands linger over his big sexy body while the water got warm.

"No amount of cleaning can cover up this dirty, sugar." His mouth fused to mine, kissing me deep and hard until my body slowly came to life just as he wanted. Lasso liked to torture me during sex, pleasing me for so damn long until I was just angry and ready to come. I hated it as much as I loved it. And him.

"That's okay, I like you dirty." And then he lifted me up and my legs went around his waist, lining our bodies up perfectly and quickly so I was against the bathroom wall, impaled on his thick cock. "Lasso, fuck."

He flashed that sexy grin that had me clenching around him, already close to coming. It was hard and fast as we swirled out of control while the steam from the shower built around us. We came on a roar, still too hungry for each other to do anything but seek out the burning desire simmering within both of us.

The same thing happened in the shower and then the bedroom, only we didn't make it to the bed. I turned and gripped the dresser, tempting him with the curve of my ass. I squealed like a cheerleader when his cock invaded me from behind, pumping hard and fast as he could, one hand gently resting on the curve of my belly while the other tweaked my nipples. It was hot. It was totally fucking insane and intense as hell, and I couldn't get enough.

"Shit, babe. You're so fucking wet."

"Been thinkin' about you all day," I told him, flashing a smile over my shoulder. And that was all it took for him to come the second time. I was moving towards a new personal best record with Lasso.

He picked me up and we fell on the bed together, his body falling first to protect me and the baby. Because this was a swoon-worthy guy. It didn't matter that he was a biker and a veteran or that he occasionally had to do fucked up things in the name of his brothers. None of it mattered when I looked at him and saw my blue-eyed badass with the messy blond hair.

"Damn girl, you sure know how to welcome a man home."

I laughed and pressed a kiss to his heart. "I want to give you something Lasso. Two things, actually, but I think you already know that you have my heart."

## Wonderfully Wrecked

He sucked in a breath that told me he hadn't known, at least not for sure.

"I love you Lasso. You've had my heart for months and I was too chicken to tell you, but I'm telling you now. I love you."

"Thank fuck! I thought I was going to have to lock you in the basement," he growled and held me tighter.

"We don't have a basement."

"Shut up," he laughed and kissed me long and hard, flipping our positions so his long, thick cock was pressed between my thighs. "Let me enjoy hearing the woman I love finally tell me she loves me, too."

I looked at him and he stared back. "Go on, tell me."

I laughed but it was no hardship to sing my love from the rooftops, because I finally understood the expression. That's exactly how I felt, like I wanted to tell the whole fucking world about this really great thing I'd found.

"I love you, Lasso. I lo-ove you!" The words kept coming but they were more garbled and difficult to understand as his tongue laved me, licked and sucked me until I tugged on his hair and pushed up against his mouth. The things he did with his tongue were magical and the thought was kind of intoxicating, that if all went well I'd be privy to that magic forever.

His tongue fucked me, licked me and brought me to the pinnacle of pleasure before he finally let me fall but not without his big strong arms there to catch me. "Holy fuck that was beautiful."

My body shook with laughter and my heart filled with happiness. "That was so incredible I almost forgot."

"The second thing?"

I nodded. "The second thing."

He stared down at me with a loving look as his fingers stroked inside of me. "Don't keep me waiting, sweetheart."

"You have my heart Lasso, but I've been pretty stupid with it over the years, giving it to dicks like Genesis. So I want to give you something no one else has ever had."

His blue eyes flashed with heat at my words and he leaned forward, kissing my mouth while his fingers did very dirty things to me. Lasso managed to wring another orgasm from me using nothing but his fingers and his kiss, using the juices to rub around my asshole. "You sure about this? You don't have to prove anything to me, babe."

"I know, and I want to do this. I want to experience this with you." His middle finger slipped into the forbidden hole and I gasped but it was surprise, not pain. And maybe a little discomfort.

"How in the hell did I get so lucky?"

"You knocked up the right girl?" My back arched, and I leaned into him.

"Damn right I did," he groaned and slid another wet finger inside me where I already felt full. His hands gripped my hips and pulled. I was on my knees and elbows as his tongue skidded up my back. I shivered. His touch was everything to me, fueling me towards pleasure while keeping me firmly where he wanted me. Underneath him.

Then his cock was there, perched at my opening and my heart thundered against my chest, so loud I was sure it had to wake the baby. It was a weird thought to have in the moment so I squashed it and focused instead on Lasso. The blunt tip of his cock sliding into my ass, one finger keeping me as slick as possible while his thick cock invaded me.

"Oh, God," I groaned and winced at the painful pleasure. "Fuck, that's good."

He groaned out my name and it was tight on his lips like he was using every bit of self-control he had not to just ram into me, not to fuck me like he really wanted to. "Shit, Rocky. So. Tight."

"Virgin asshole remember?"

## Wonderfully Wrecked

He growled and slid deeper until he was fully inside. "Oh fuck!"

And suddenly the discomfort was so insignificant I barely noticed it as pleasure took over, the thick push and pull of his cock was a tempting sensation that had me pushing back against him, begging for more. I wanted all of him. Pounding into my ass like a jackhammer. My asshole opened up to him, as his strokes grew faster and deeper, his breathing shallow and harsh as he sought his pleasure.

And mine. His hand slid around my hip and down between my legs and he played with my clit as he fucked my ass, creating so many sensations that I couldn't even focus.

The sensation began at the tips of my toenails and slowly worked its way across my whole body, his cock and fingers controlling me. When Lasso allowed it, the orgasm moved up my body and worked its way to the surface. When he wanted me to cry out, I did.

It was a heady sensation that made me feel one time I did LSD in the desert. Colors were everywhere, and my body vibrated as if every particle that made me a person was humming independently.

"More," I moaned and pushed against him again, harder.

"Fuck yeah," he growled, smacking my ass twice in a flash, and thrusting deeper. Harder. So deep that when he pinched my clit I went off like an animal in heat, orgasm roaring through me with the power of a runaway train. My orgasm triggered his and his teeth clamped down on my shoulder as his hot load shot into my ass.

He grunted, "Fuck. Me." His body jerked a few times and then he pulled out of me slowly and rolled over, pulling me with him. "Rocky, babe, I love the hell out of you."

I smiled and turned to face him. "I love you too, cowboy."

"I know." He waggled his eyebrows as only he could.

"By the way, that doesn't count as one of my surprises."

"There are more?"

I nodded over to the painting leaning against the armoire in the corner. He stood and fell back on the bed, laughing because his legs were still shaky from our all out love binge. Then he tried again, barely made it this time and somehow staggered to the large painting while I giggled at him. He turned it around and stared for so long I was certain he hated it. I'd drawn and then painted it from memory. Lasso, shirtless with a cigarette hanging from his lips, his Reckless Bastards vest hanging from a finger over his back, his gorgeous face in profile. It looked like a man who didn't want to leave his woman, looking back at her with love and desire in his eyes.

"Damn Rocky, that's incredible." He looked at me, smiling like a big kid. "You did this?"

I nodded, shy and proud.

"You really do love me."

"Thought we covered that already, cowboy. Try to keep up here."

I watched his big body eat up the short steps back to bed with a predatory gleam in his eyes. "That painting is magnificent. I feel like I need a new house and new furniture just to hang it up."

"You're kidding, right? It'll go perfect right above the sofa on that wall. I would have had it hung before you got home but this belly proved to be too big an obstacle."

"Don't say that. I love your belly." To prove it, he pressed a kiss so soft it brought a tear to my eye. When he looked up, Lasso's blue eyes were suspiciously wet, but I didn't comment on it. "Anything else?"

I laughed and pushed at his chest. "You're a greedy fucker, aren't you?"

"When it comes to you? All day, every fucking day, babe."

## Wonderfully Wrecked

"My asshole hurts," I said, but I laughed. "I've never felt so fucking high, though. Think we can do it again sometime?"

"Fuck, yeah, we can. I'll take your ass anytime you want. But you might wanna go clean up. Butt-fucking can get kind of messy."

"Not moving from here. I'm too fucking boneless." I kissed his collarbone. "You smell good."

His hand went to my ass and squeezed. "That's all you, babe. Flowers and sex."

"There's one more thing," I told him. He was supposed to show up for my appointment earlier today but had obviously been busy getting a busted-up lip.

"I already know you love me."

"Good because that's not it. Since you never ever use it, I think we should name our son, Dallas."

He sucked in a breath and those baby blue eyes turned dark blue, smooth like velvet and I couldn't look away.

"Boy? We're having a boy," he said, voice filled with awe. "A boy. Dallas."

"You said that already."

"Give me a moment, woman. It's not every day a man finds out his first born will be a boy."

I knew he would be emotional about it because underneath his big bad biker, ex-military badass thing was the heart of a softy. I loved that damn softy.

"You'll be a great daddy."

His shoulders sagged in relief. "Fuck, yeah, I will."

"I can't wait to see you hold our son in your arms."

He smiled and smacked a kiss against my lips. "I guess we owe Big Boy a debt of gratitude. If he hadn't been grabbing you that night, you might have left before I got a chance to hit on you."

"Maybe you should thank Baby Dallas, since he's the reason I showed up on your doorstep."

"Babe, I don't give a damn if it was the devil himself that gave me a second chance with you, I'll always be grateful. You're the best thing that's happened to me in a long time and I can't wait to start our life together."

I wrapped my arms around his neck and grinned. "Together starts now, baby."

\* \* \* \*

# ~ THE END ~

## Acknowledgements

Thank you so much for making my books a success! I appreciate all of you! Thanks to all of my beta readers, street teamers, ARC readers and Facebook fans. Y'all are THE BEST!

And a huge very special thanks to Jessie! I'm such a *hot mess, but without your keen sense of organization and skills, I'd be a burny fiery inferno of hot mess!! Thank you!

And a very special thanks to my editors (who sometimes have to work all through the night! *See HOT MESS above!) Thank you for making my words make sense.

Copyright © 2018 KB Winters and BookBoyfriends Publishing LLC

KB Winters

## About The Author

KB Winters is a Wall Street Journal and USA Today Bestselling Author of steamy hot books about Bikers, Billionaires, Bad Boys and Badass Military Men. Just the way you like them. She has an addiction to caffeine, tattoos and hard-bodied alpha males. The men in her books are very sexy, protective and sometimes bossy, her ladies are…well…*bossier*!

Living in sunny Southern California, with her five kids and three fur babies, this embarrassingly hopeless romantic writes every chance she gets!

You can reach me at Facebook.com/kbwintersauthor and at kbwintersauthor@gmail.com

Copyright © 2018 KB Winters and BookBoyfriends Publishing LLC

Printed in Great Britain
by Amazon